I0538557

OPEN

WOUND

Things Can Get Bloody..
When The Past Comes Calling

Author Jason Beckett

OPEN WOUND

Copyright © 2015 Jason Beckett

All rights reserved. No part of this book may be reproduced or transmitted in any form or by any means, electronic or mechanical, including photocopying, recording, or by any information storage and retrieval system, without permission in writing from the publisher. All questions and/or request are to be submitted to: 134 Andrew Drive, Reidsville NC, 27320.

To the best of said publisher's knowledge, this is an original manuscript and is the sole property of author **JASON BECKETT**

Printed in the United States of America

ISBN-13:978-0692511091
ISBN-10:0692511091

Printed by Createspace 2015
Published by BlaqRayn Publishing Plus 2015

DEDICATION

First and foremost I must give all praises to God and Him alone for my existence, my mind, and my family. Without God's intervention within my life I wouldn't been strong enough to withstand the many trials I went through throughout my past and present lifetime. Also for the gift to write beautiful poetry and create stories that turn into books for the lovely readers out there.

I thank my mother, my lifeline, my heart and soul Ms. Leslie Beckett. I thank God for allowing you to be still here as your son live his dream, and for being a great woman of strength to raise my siblings and I all by your lonesome, thank you for being a mother who gave me love in the only way you knew how. I love you with God's type of love.

To my grandmother(rip) Edith Becks, I know you're resting upon the throne that God prepared just for you. You are a pillar in my life today, because I carry your loving spirit deep within the epitome of my soul. The values that you taught me as a young teenager that I didn't take heed to then, I now apply to my life now with great success, you were always a God fearing woman, I love you forever.

To my father Brooklyn C. Smith, you weren't in my life during my childhood as you should of been to teach me how to grow into a man, but you not being there built great strength in me, and God loved me through my faults so I must love you through yours, I love you for giving me life.

To my dear Uncle Ashby Beckett, Aunt Edna Burns, Aunt Williemae Drummond, Granddaddy Boots, Aunt Cookie- I love and miss you, Cousins Honey, Olie, Vedri Cocker(C.C.), Aunt Shirley Hawkins, to all of you (R.I.P.) in heaven to you all, you are deeply missed but never forgotten.

Curtis Lee Hawkins(r.i.p.), cousin and one of my best friends, there's no words in the world that could explain the pain I carried through life from your not being here, but God healed my heart and you live within it, you were the best man, one love forever koondingy.

To my niece Kiara Beckett(keeblaq), niece NaAdra Beckett, niece NaShawn Smiley,nephew Steven Hopskins(lil Steve), nephews Wisdom Marshall, Obadiah Marshall, Blessed Marshall, Kingdom Marshall, my great niece NiAsia Hopskins, great niece Journee, great nephews Jaden and Jordan(the twins), I love you all unconditionally, and I'm writing for you all future, what I do is for you.

To my family, The Beckett's, The Becks, The Burns, The Drummonds, The Smiths, The Halls, The Faulks, The Diggs, The South's, The Bonney Family(Tina),Kim Cohcran, Torrey Cohcran, and any I may have not named I love you with my complete existence.

To BlaqRayn BRPP NETWORK CEO Ms. Kim Morrow, I thank you for everything, because of you I'm about to leak all the ink out of my every pen, let's work. Your professionalism, grind, hard work, vision, and outlooks, along with flaming book covers inspire me each and everyday to push even harder to give readers books of enjoyment, and poetry that would light a match in one single strike, Let's Work.

To the BRPP family, glad to be among you all, let's give these readers flames of fire to read.

To the loving readers who purchase and read us writers, author's, poets work and books, I openly thank you for continuing to give me, us, a job that we so love to do, because of you all we have a job, because of your undying support we're able to eat.

To all of the author's before me thank you for giving me a platform as well as great books to read as well.

To the present day author's, thank you for keeping our platform alive, to my Author Family who are great friends and supports I thank you.

To the late great Queen Ms. Maya Angelou, you were the best example of a poet, icon, and human being to me. Your poetry helped me to dig deep within myself and write the best true poetry I could possibly write, thank you for thank you for sharing you with us(rest in peace, in my heart, and in heaven).

Author Christine Davis, I thank you deeply, you being the young great writer you are really inspires me so ever more you just don't know, can't wait for us to write many nooks together in the near future little niece. Dion Antoinette Wallace-Davis and husband, you have a strong young queen, and thanks for being fam, don't worry I got her.

My Extended Fam: Ms. Fanita Moon Pendleton(my right hand), Racquel Williams, Ebonee Oliver, Stacy Thomas, Papaya Wagstaff, Ambria Davis, Adrienne Cunningham, Ambria Davis, Caroline Bates, Esarc Winterz, Raggae(lil man), Bally(Power House brother), Jay and sis Tasha, Rick W. , Paul Asbelle, Issac Wells, Booga and Bunny, and many of my Park Place fam, thanks for always holding me down and being the truth.

Last but not least, to my LAMBERT'S POINT and PARK PLACE family, we are in the building and we are here to build a platform let's work, one love to the neighborhoods that helped raised me, we are one family...Norfolk, Virginia.

OPEN

WOUND

Things Can Get Bloody..
When The Past Comes Calling

Author Jason Beckett

Chapter One

It's August 16, 2006 and Lorenzo Barnes is in his cell sitting on his bunk waiting to be released from state prison after serving a ten year sentence. His cellmate Z-man walks in,

"Yo Zo, it's almost that time ace, around 5:00 pm we'll be grubbing on that chow, but you'll be grubbing on some of that good warm wet coochie out there in the free world..."

"...Make sure that coochie fresh and clean ace. I don't want to hear you walking around the hood looking like you been in a brawl with Iron Mike Tyson, lips all swollen and shit from your face being in between somebody's momma legs all night eating some bad shit" Z-man added.

Lorenzo responded, " yeah you right, what time yo momma get home from work again."

Z-man rushed up to Lorenzo hit him with a few playful jabs to his rib-cage then dapped him up along with a brotherly hug and began.

"Yo Zo,stay free man, you know these devils ain't playing up in here dog. They giving out football numbers now, you see all these kids coming up in this joint with fifty and sixty years, just go out there and live ace. "

"For sure dog, no way I'm coming back up in this hell hole, I'm giving myself a chance at life real talk, as soon as these kats about to get released they talking about I'm going out there get a job, find a good girl, take care of my seeds, start a business, and thirty days later you hear they back up in the jail on their way back to the pen", Lorenzo explained.

"Go home and take care of ma' dukes you feel me ace, you only get one", Z-man advised.

"Being away from her been painful dog, don't think I would of made it through without her letters, love, and support; she kept me in check, plus you know mom's a prosecutor. She would kick my ass sho'nuff if I get caught up in some more bullshit", Lorenzo stated.

"Plus, I gots to utilize some of my time to comfort all of my tenderonies that kept daddy time well occupied with countless letters and pics, anything else would be uncivilized", Lorenzo added.

Z-man replied,"yeah, that's why yo ass stayed creeping to the bat cave late at night with them pics when you thought niggas were asleep with your backed up ass", then laughed out loud.

"Yo ass backed up to home slice, but guess what, call yo momma later on tonight and when you gets no answer just know ya boy ain't backed up no more", Lorenzo taunted then started laughing.

Z-man blurted out, "eat shit man I hate yo ass", then laughed and went on to say, "well at least tell her that I sent the dick; maybe you can beat that coochie up and get some paper put on my books cause she ain't sent a nigga shit."

Lorenzo burst into laughter and stated, "man yo ass wild, but you keeps it real, that's why I fucks with you major ace."

While Lorenzo and Z-man were chopping it up, a prison guard shouted out loudly,

"Lorenzo Barnes your rides here, you ain't got to go but you gots to get the hell up out of here."

Lorenzo gave Z-man dap and said, " I'm a hold you down ace", then turned, walked off and he was on his way.

Lorenzo had no bags just the letters and pictures he decided to keep, they were sealed inside of a 8 by 10 inch Manila envelope, all but the recent letter he received from his mother. He kept that letter in his back pocket just in case he wanted to read it again. It filled him with joy whenever he read it. He left everything else he had to Z-man.

When Lorenzo walked through and outside the prison gates, he didn't look back, he just wanted to get as far away from Buckingham Correctional Center as he possibly could. Mr. Chambers, a prison guard was waiting inside a van outside the entrance of the prison to drive Lorenzo to the Greyhound Bus Station. The prison had purchased his bus ticket home the day before and given it to him upon his release. He also was given a check for 2700.00 dollars, the money he had saved up on his personal prison account, and 25.00 in cash the prison gives to anyone being released.

Just as Lorenzo reached to open the van's middle sliding door, Mr. Chambers hollered out..

"Hop up front here, you a free man now Mr. Barnes." Lorenzo did, buckling up when he was seated. He stared out the window as they passed giant fields of grassy farmland with bundles of hay and cattle, he smiled and silently thanked God for his freedom.

"Where's home, where you heading Mr. Barnes", Mr.Chambers asked.

Lorenzo replied, "Norfolk, Virginia and I can't wait to get there either."

Mr. Chambers babbled on..

"I been to Newport News, Virginia but never to Norfolk."

Lorenzo responded with laugh and commented.

"Then you've been to Norfolk because they're one in the same."

"So, how does it feel to be free after ten years? You know a lot has changed out here in the world since you've been inside", stated Mr. Chambers.

"You mean since my being released from within the belly of the beast as we call it. I'm just happy to be reuniting with my mother and the world. I may be free but physically I'm still in the devil's domain", Lorenzo answered.

In prison, Lorenzo was a bad ass. He would fight in a minute if he felt threatened; he took no shit from no one, big or small. The fellas labeled him "trained to go" because he had plenty of heart and would throw them hands in a second.

As months and years passed , he met Brother James, a Muslim brother who was a member of the Nation of Islam. Brother James took a liking to

Lorenzo, together they walked almost daily around the prison rec yard talking about life while Brother James also explained to him who Allah(God) was, and how Allah transformed his life over the years. He actually was the one who helped Lorenzo clean up his physical appearance, and helped him to acquire knowledge of himself and life. Lorenzo was grateful for all that Brother James did for him.

Suddenly Mr. Chambers interrupted Lorenzo thoughts.

" You want to stop somewhere to get you a bite to eat, get some soul grease on them bones", asked Mr. Chambers.

Lorenzo replied,"no sir, I'm good. I just want to get home and as far away from Buckingham as I can before they have a recall on all Lorenzos."

Mr. Chambers laughed out loud and said,

"I ain't heard that one before, well okay, destination Greyhound Bus Station it is."

A short while later they pulled into the Greyhound Bus Station parking lot in Richmond, Virginia. Lorenzo looked around at all the people moving about, at the nice clothing some wore, but especially at all the fine, thick, bootylicious chicks he saw at every angle.

"Well, this is your stop Mr. Barnes, take care and enjoy your freedom, value it", announced Mr. Chambers.

Lorenzo replied, "thank you sir, and I will." He exited the van, shutting the door behind him.

Lorenzo walked to the entrance of the station, went in and stood in line waiting to reach the help center desk for information on the bus he'd traveling home on. He looked around the station until the desk clerk said, "next in line please.

Lorenzo walked up to the desk..

"Hello, I wanted to know what bus I'd be boarding for Norfolk, Virginia?"

The desk clerk asked,.

"Sir, do you have a bus ticket and if so, may I see it please?"

Lorenzo handed her his ticket, waiting as she typed something in her computer.

The clerk then advised Lorenzo, "your bus will arrive at door #8 approximately 11:15am scheduled arrival time."

Lorenzo replied, "thank you and enjoy the rest of your day," turning to walk away.

He looked at the clock on the wall, realizing he had two hours until the arrival of his bus, so he took a seat in the waiting area next to a young lady who was reading a book. She didn't even look up as he sat down; she was that deep into her read. Lorenzo, himself a reader, thought that book must be some fire because she is locked into it hard! He leaned over to get a peek at the title, seeing it was one by Zane he'd read in prison.

At that instant, she looked up at Lorenzo and voiced.

"Excuse me sir, may I help you? Did you lose something over here?"

Lorenzo apologized, "sorry..."

"...I noticed that you were so deep into that book I wanted to see what it was you were reading. Now I know why you were so deeply focused... Purple Panties, that book will do something to you."

She started laughing and asked, "how do you know?"

Lorenzo smiled her way.

"Cause I read it while I was in prison along with many other books."

"From the looks of it. being that you got all them muscles popping out making that white beater look real good on. you proves where you been," she stated.

Lorenzo answered her, "it does huh?"

She replied, "I just got out myself."

"Wow, I wouldn't even have guessed that, but anyway, my name is Lorenzo, nice to meet you".

She responded, "nice to meet you, my name is not interested" then burst into laughter at the expression on Lorenzo's face.

Lorenzo looked at her in amazement and she said, "smile... I'm just kidding with.. you have a sense of humor, damn."

Lorenzo proclaimed, "what... you better be."

"I better be what? "

Lorenzo replied, "thinking about how much you want all of this" then started laughing at the expression on her face.

"Don't get full of yourself now, but you are cute and your body um um um...can I touch it?" she asked.

Lorenzo commented, "sure, as long as you don't bite it."

She reached over, running her hand all over Lorenzo's arms and chest as she began getting moist between her thighs. She hadn't had any sexual gratification with a man in five years and right now, she was beyond horny. She wanted to feel Lorenzo's hardness inside her and now before it was too late.

Lorenzo mentioned, "I still don't know your name."

"My name is Alisha, now come with me and keep up."

Lorenzo followed in her tracks and couldn't help but notice that juicy, round bubble of an ass she had in them tight fitting khakis. He got a hard on just looking at it, but he was still wondering where they were headed.

Alisha ignored Lorenzo til they reached the station's storage closet. She looked around to make sure no one was in sight then checked to see if the storage room door was unlock; it was. She then grabbed his hand, opened the door, pulling him inside with her as she locked the door behind them. Inside she backed him up against the wall, attempting to kiss him on his lips, but Lorenzo stopped her, whispering, "no lips."

Alisha whispered back "okay", licking him on his neck and nibbling his ear with one hand massaging his manhood through his shorts. Lorenzo grabbed her ass with both hands, rubbing and squeezing, murmuring...

"Damn yo ass soft as shit."

Alisha felt his manhood become rock hard and was in amazement of its length she felt through the shorts he wore. She began unbuckling his belt, then unbuttoned his shorts, zipping them all the way down. She put her hand down inside his boxers and grabbed hold of his dagger. She began stroking his pipe, at times stopping only to gently massage his sack. Lorenzo moaned softly as he continued to rub on Alisha's soft firm sitting muscle. Alisha whispered in Lorenzo's ear,

"I'm going to taste this dick then I want it in me and you better fuck me good."

Alisha went down on her knees, sliding both Lorenzo's shorts and boxers down with her. She held Lorenzo's pipe up with one hand and began licking and sucking all over his sack, stopping only to engulf the entire sack in her mouth, causing Lorenzo to groan in deep pleasure. She then traced her tongue up his shaft until reaching its head; she slowly took it into her warm mouth.

Lorenzo placed one hand softly on her head as she took his pipe deeper into her mouth, one inch at a time, until it was hidden deep in her throat and covered in warm saliva. Lorenzo's face bunched up like he had a mouth hull of sour candy as he stood there motionless.

"My father", Lorenzo somehow strained the words out in a hoarse, crackling tone.

Alisha stopped, stood up, the no kissing rule went straight out the window as Lorenzo devoured her mouth with his. Seconds later, she pushed him back and looked straight into his eyes. He then grabbed her, turned her around ass faced against him, kissing and sucking on her neck as she rested her head against his chest. Lorenzo slid his hands up her shirt, unsnapped her bra and caught her soft round tits as they dropped into his hands. He massaged her nipples, squeezing and teasing her tits repeatedly until he could resist no longer.

Lorenzo reached around, unbuttoned Alisha's pants, sliding them and her panties down to her ankles. Alisha bent forward, grabbing hold to the sink in front of her and spread her legs apart about eleven inches. Lorenzo slowly guided his pipe inside her, knowing her sweet spot would be tight and would have to open to his size. Once inside, he gave her slow deep, strokes.

Alisha had to stuff her own shirt in her mouth to silence her love cries. The more he stroked, the more she opened up to drown his shaft in her wet, hot ocean. Gripping her waist tightly, he slowly stroked her sweet spot until she cried out in ecstasy, knowing she was spreading her warm cream all over his shaft.that's He then delivered deep barbarian like strokes to her ocean's floor until he himself exploded and released his full load inside her. They both stood there stiff and winded until they caught their breaths.

"Damn nigga that dick was so on point, but you tried to bust a chick ovaries, you forgot I'm just getting out too."

They both looked at each other and burst into laughter.

Lorenzo answered, "I apologize. I apologize for not touching your soul with this pipe."

Alisha laughed then babbled, "go to hell Lorenzo."

Lorenzo assured her, "I just left the place."

Alisha just shook her head as they both got dressed.

"We got to hurry up..I ain't trying to miss my bus although I would love to take you and that golden globe winner hanging down inside them shorts of yours home with me, cause together we all could do some thangs" Alisha quipped as she smiled devilishly at Lorenzo.

Alisha peeked out the door to see if anyone was around, it was clear so she and Lorenzo quickly returned to the waiting area, taking their seats. Their timing was perfect! Twenty minutes later Lorenzo's bus pulled in and announced passengers boarding to report to door #8 with their tickets.

"Well that's my ride" Lorenzo declared as he stood to make his way to door #8.

Alisha stood, gave Lorenzo a hug and replied "damn I should of got your info to keep in touch..maybe even come see you."

Before Lorenzo could respond, they made called last call for passengers.

Lorenzo hissed..

"Damn! Sorry I gotta go.. can't miss my bus.

Take care and be safe."

Then he was gone.

Alisha watched intently as his bus began to pull away from the station,thinking to herself she should have gotten his information from the beginning.

"I think your friend that just left dropped his letter in the seat" the lady sitting two seats over was handing her a folded envelope.

Alisha reached out to accept the letter from her and replied..

"Thank you, I'm sure he would be looking for this. I'll make sure to let him know you found it and gave it to me."

Alisha pulled the letter from the open envelope, curious as to whom it may be from and saw on the last page *Love, your mother. Can't wait until my son comes home*. Alisha smiled. She now had a way of contacting Lorenzo.

Suddenly, they announced all passengers awaiting bus #3 to get ready for boarding, the bus was pulling in. Alisha got in line and when it was her time, she gave the doorman her ticket; destination, her home, New York City.

Chapter Two

Sitting by the window on the bus, as it traveled down the interstate heading to Norfolk, Virginia, Lorenzo relaxed looking at all the scenery. He imagined the expression on his mother's face when she opened the door to see him standing there. He also wondered if any of the friends he grew up with were still around. He knew so much had changed since his incarceration.

A vision of Alisha and the sexual encounter they'd just had rushed him, flooding his thoughts. Damn, he thought to himself, that coochie was wetter than the ocean itself... tight and some kind of good! Shit! Why my dumb ass ain't at least get her number. Could've been like me taking a little vacation going to visit her sometime since I've never been to New York. Well, guess it's a little too late to think about it now anyway...

xxxxxxxxxxxxxxx

Alisha sat back in her seat smiling, replaying over and over the sex she and Lorenzo had just little while ago.

Damn, that nigga served that wood to my ass like it was the last time he was ever going to see me, then again it might be, but not if it's up to me she thought.

Alisha couldn't help but think about how Lorenzo's hands had felt on her bare skin when he was rubbing and squeezing her tits and ass. She decided to just close her eyes and let her thoughts travel to wherever they choose to go...

xxxxxxxxxxxxx

After two hours of uncomfortable riding, the driver on Lorenzo's bus announced over the intercom..

"We are now pulling up to Greyhound Station Norfolk..please remain seated until the bus comes to a complete stop then at that time, you may exit your bus and retrieve your luggage with the help of Greyhound Staff awaiting to assist you outside at the luggage area. Please watch your step as you exit the bus, have a great day and thank you for choosing Greyhound."

Lorenzo's heart began to race from the pure excitement of being free and knowing in just a short time he would be wrapping his arms around his mother for the first time in ten long, hard and very stressful years. He imagined the look on her face when she opened the door to his knock and wondered if he'd be shedding more tears than her.

He simply smiled to himself; there was no way to prepare for that meeting. All the home cooked family meals with just the two of them, things he'd thought of while in prison, were all about to come into fruition soon enough.

Knowing he had his mother thinking he came home next month was his way of surprising her, making this the greatest day of his life he thought. His mother still lived in Park Place, in the same house she bought when he was a kid and before he went to prison. It was only a twenty-minute walk so he got to stepping that instant he grabbed his small bag.

As Lorenzo traveled home down Granby Street, he noticed a lot had changed, but the old Brass Pawn Shop was still standing strong. It brought back memories of him and his childhood friend Curtis stealing a Pink Beach cruiser Bike to get back home to Norfolk from Chesapeake after an overnight stay at some chicks house. Lorenzo was the driver while Curtis sat comfy on the handlebars.

When they reached Norfolk turning on Granby Street, they were about to ride past Brass Pawn Shop, but decided to stop in just to see what they had. They left the beach cruiser outside by the door on its kickstand. After about 10 minutes, they returned to find the beach cruiser gone.

Curtis was stunned, "yo somebody stole the Pink Panther.." that was the name given the beach cruiser.

Mad at first, they figured "oh well" and started walking home. They reached the train tracks and Lorenzo looked to my left to see if a train was coming then to my right, and, low and behold what did he see but a man crossing the tracks on the Pink Panther a block down from where they stood.

Lorenzo hollered out " hey, Curtis, follow me... I see the Pink Panther."

Lorenzo ran fast, turning left at the first block he came to with Curtis right on his heels. They noticed the man riding the bike had stopped and was doing something to one of the tires then got back on, starting to peddle, but it was a little too late. He didn't see Lorenzo coming as he closed-lined the man with such brute force his body did a full backwards flip off of the bike and he landed hard on the concrete. At that point, Lorenzo and Curtis beat and stomped the man until they just decided to stop, hopped on the beach cruiser and got out of dodge.

The crazy thing about it, Lorenzo now reflected, was they'd whipped that man's ass over a bike they'd stolen and he stole from them. They both knew they were lucky the cops hadn't been called by someone in a passing vehicle watching as they beat the man to a pulp. However, they'd made it home safe and nothing ever came from that incident. Lorenzo laughed and shook his head at those crazy times. Curtis was now resting in peace with God. He'd been shot and killed by one of two guys who attempted to rob him a few months before Lorenzo went to prison.

"Hey you, is every muscle you got swole like the ones on your arms and chest", a chic hollered out from a group of females standing by a car talking in a Taco Bell restaurant parking lot as he walked by, immediately snapping Lorenzo back to reality.

Lorenzo smiled, responding loudly.

"Oh yeah.. and like during a workout, they all get hard as steel.."

The entire group of girls all said in unison..

"Damnnnn! "

The girl who'd first yelled out now asked..

"Well can a sistah get them digits or do I have to come kidnap yo ass?"

Lorenzo stopped dead in his tracks, pointing out to her..

"Well looks like you need to get yo lil sexy self to moving them feet cause if you want it so bad, you come get it."

The other girls whispered to their friend, "girl you better get that number before I do and that ain't no lie." As she began walking towards Lorenzo, his eyes was locked in on that beauty.

Lorenzo mumbled to himself in the Crocodile Hunter voice "she's a beauty..."

He couldn't take his eyes off of her! She had a face and body like Lisa Raye and a bow-legged walk like Nia Long; he was smiling concrete hard.

And, her ass he thought, I gots to get with that. Deep stroke back shots are a must!"

" Hello there handsome I'm Angelica" she spoke as she stopped two feet in front of him.

"Hello Angelica... nice to meet you, I'm Lorenzo."

"So Lorenzo, my guess is you're coming from the gym with all those muscles popping out and waving at me?"

Smiling extra hard Lorenzo stating, "well actually, I'm just coming home from prison, but nice pick up line", he added with a laugh."

"Well in that case, allow to be the first to welcome you home."

She hugged Lorenzo, rubbing her hands up and down his arms, murmuring..

"Um.. Um ..um," to herself as she felt the muscles ripple and pulse under her fingertips.

Lorenzo grinned, "hey now, I usually charge a fee for touching all of this masculinity, but I'm a give you a pass today just cause you're beautiful and that body is oh so delicious."

Angelica burst into laughter, replying..

"Thank you, you're funny, but know that I give out the passes mister."

Lorenzo answered with a salute.

"Yes ma'am Sergeant feisty lady."

Angelica laughed; it seemed to be some private joke until she spoke again and all became clear.

"Uhm...funny you should say that, considering I actually am a Sergeant with the Norfolk Police Department..."

Lorenzo eyes grew wider than 50 cent pieces; Angelica couldn't contain her amusement.

Angelica blurted out..

"Oh so what, you nervous now?" Angelica teased Lorenzo.

"Cat got your tongue? Meow! Guess you ain't liking me no more now huh?"

Lorenzo laughed and said,

"You really ain't right for that shit you just said. Yes it alarmed me, but you know what? Come on and handcuff me, sexy… I'll be your prisoner. Hold me captive inside ALL of your walls."

Angelica laughed. "You so nasty Lorenzo."

"Wait a minute….isn't it against your job's rules and regulations to be in any type of relationship with a convicted felon?" Lorenzo asked, slightly concerned.

"Who says there's going to be a 'relationship' and not just 'relations'?" she replied with a devilish smirk. "And anyway, IF it becomes an issue, I'll deal with it when the time comes."

"Truuuuu…." Lorenzo nodded. "Well baby, I wish I could stay and chat it up with you, but I'm anxious to see my wonderful mother. She thinks I'm not coming home til next month so she's going to be really surprised."

"Awww, I can tell you're a sweetheart Lorenzo," Angelica swooned. "So can a chick give you her digits so maybe we can get to know each other better? In a more appropriate way and under a better setting?" Angelica asked.

"Sure, that would be nice," he smiled.

"Ok hold on a sec…..let me go get some pen and paper right quick. Don't you go NO where Mr. Sexy."

"I ain't going nowhere," Lorenzo promised.

"I'mma just be sitting right here checking out that bone structure as you walk off."

Angelica just laughed and shook her head as she walked away.

Lorenzo shook his own head as he intensely watched her body movements like he was focused on the Super Bowl.

When Angelica returned, she pressed a pink sticky note firmly in the palm of his hand.

"Here's my number. You'd want to memorize it like your life depended on it, okay?" she cooed.

"Show you right," Lorenzo replied, licking his lips.

Chapter Three

Alisha's bus finally arrived at the Greyhound Station in New York. She was so relieved and so ready to get the hell off that stinky ass bus. The ride was damn near unbearable but the banging sex she had with Lorenzo made it all well worth it.

"Damn, that wood felt like it was moving mountains up inside of me," she reminisced, smiling to herself. "Okay Alisha snap yo horny ass back to reality RIGHT now!" She giggled.

Suddenly the driver of the bus came over the intercom.

"Those of you who are departing us here in New York, make sure you retrieve your luggage and baggage from the baggage area of the bus," he announced. "Please watch your step upon exiting and thank you for riding with Greyhound."

As Alisha stepped down from the bus, she watched loved ones embracing passengers who were getting off and she felt a sharp pain in her chest. Her mother had been involved in an horrific car crash and passed away while she was serving time in prison, and the only man she knew as a father figure was serving a life sentence with no chance of parole in Federal prison. The only family Alisha had left that she had contact with at all was her best friend from childhood, Sasha.

Alisha! Alisha!" She turned in the direction of the voice screaming her name and lo and behold, it was her best friend Sasha, walking towards her smiling.

They hugged so tight it seemed as though they were trying to disappear inside of each other.

"Damn girl I missed you!" Sasha gushed, then stepped back to get a full look at Alisha.

"Girrrl....you got thick up in there I see! Ass like Serena Williams!"

Alisha burst out laughing. "I'm soooo glad to see you too boo! And yes hunny, I got ass for days now, AND it's soft!"

Sasha smacked her on the ass and it gave a little bounce.

"Damn! I might have to get that ass up in the club with me so you can rake in major paper! Them tricks would love that shit!" Sasha teased.

Alisha turned her back to Sasha and bounced her ass up and down. "More bounce to the ounce baby!"

Sasha laughed and said, "C'mon here chick, let's boogie. We gots mad catching up to do before we blaze the town tonight."

They reached the parking lot and Sasha walked over to the driver side door of a 2006 money green Jaguar.

"Daaaaaaamn girl!" Alisha squealed. "You ain't tell me you was balling like this! Yo this shit hard body!"

"Girl you know how I do and I do that shit well!" Sasha boasted, snapping her freshly French-tipped fingers. "Them dope boys make it rain when 'DREAM' is on stage!"

DREAM is Sasha's stage name at Club Gold, located in the heart of Brooklyn, where she works as the most requested exotic dancer, and Sasha's dope new ride was proof of that. It was freshly painted with gold and silver flakes in it, a sunroof and 22" rims. It was definitely beyond fly. When they got in the car, Sasha popped her Nicki Minaj CD in the deck and track 5, 'Star Chick,' banged through her speakers. As they breezed through the streets, Alisha sank deep into the beige butter-smooth leather seats and focused all her attention out the window, enjoying every minute of the hustle and bustle taking place before her eyes. She thought a lot about days like this while she was in the pen, and now….she was finally back in the midst of it. She was back home.

Before Alisha knew it, they were turning into Marcy Projects. No matter how much money she was raking in dancing, and she was really bringing in them dollars, Marcy has always been home to Sasha. She was comfortable there; she was happy there; and there she planned to always to stay. She parked her car in front of a tall apartment building around twelve stories high.

When they got out the car, Alisha took in all the sights and sounds of home and allowed it to envelope her.

"Girl I truly missed New York," she said, trying hard to swallow down any tears that were threatening to escape.

Sasha smiled at Alisha and rested her head on her shoulder. "Yup…my right hand chick is back."

Chapter Four

Lorenzo finally reached his mother's house in Norfolk, VA where he grew up. As he walked up the driveway to the door, he noticed a White Mercedes in the driveway. It was clean with a glossy shine to it, factory rims and all the extra accessories you could use to beautify a car. That was his mom…she just liked it plain and simple; new or near new.

Lorenzo looked himself over in the passenger side view mirror, then stepped up to the door and rang the bell. Seconds later he heard his mother's voice.

"Just a minute….I'll be right there!"

Lorenzo's heart was pounding; he's waited so many years for this very day.

Finally the door swung open and Lorenzo's grin stretched from one corner to the next.

"Hey mom!"

The look on her face was absolutely priceless. Tears instantly burst from her eyes as she grabbed her son and squeezed him hard, as if she would never let him out of her sight again.

Gina Mae Barnes, a retired prosecutor for the state of Virginia, was in her mid-60's. She stood about 5'5" tall, weighed around 155 pounds, had a chestnut skin tone and a low but fiery voice. In the courtroom, she was given the nickname "Lioness" because of the powerful attacks she threw during heavy crime cases; as a matter of fact, roughly 85% of the cases she was set to prosecute worked out plea bargains because nobody wanted that "rumble in the jungle."

Gina finally let go of her son, only to hug him again and plant a sloppy kiss on his cheek. Gina

Mae pulled her baby boy inside the house and shut her door.

When his mother was finally able to speak, she spoke slowly and tearfully.

"Son I stayed in prayer with God daily and nightly, asking Him to please bring you back home to me the same way you left, and I thank Him deeply for answering my prayers! Glory be to Him and only Him!"

"Mom I've missed you so much," Lorenzo replied. "Every day behind them walls all I could think of was you; praying for you, for God to keep you safe til the day I would finally be able to hug and kiss you again and tell you how much I love you, idolize you and cherish you deep within my heart and soul. You are my angel mom. Your unconditional love and devotion gave me the strength to hold firm, and changed my life for the better. The love you injected into me helped design the man you see today. YOU did this mom,"

Lorenzo finished, tears streaming down his cheeks. Gina Mae was speechless. She'd never heard her son speak of his love for her in this manner and she was numb with joy.

He wiped his face with the back of his hands and switched topics slightly.

"So mom who is this man you've been telling me about in your letters?"

She popped him lightly on his head and smiled.

"None of your business young man. But I promise you'll meet him soon enough. He always asked how you were doing and even wanted to visit you, but I wouldn't allow him to; I believed it was better for you two to meet once you finally came home. He said he'll happily answer any questions you may have for him, and even do a background check if you like. I've already handled that though," she confirmed with a stern look on her face.

Lorenzo laughed loud.

"Oh I KNOW you did mom. I think you did a background check on every friend I ever had, whether they were my cousins, your nephews, or nieces."

"You better believe it! Times two!" Gina Mae laughed.

"Oh!" she suddenly said, very excited. "I want to show you some pictures I accumulated over the years that you were incarcerated," she said jumping up from the couch.

"Yes ma'am," Lorenzo smiled, leaning his head back on the sofa while he waited on his mother to return.

Chapter Five

As Alisha and Sasha reached the front entrance of the building, three guys were seated out on the stoop; one of them spoke.

"Hey Sasha, you looking like a fresh crisp one hundred dollar bill."

"Hey Deadline, you looking like a bag of copper pennies. I should just take yo ass upstairs with me and drop yo ass in my change jar," Sasha shot back.

Alisha let out a thunder of laughter and Deadline and the rest of the crew couldn't help but laugh too.

"I hate yo crazy ass."

Sasha giggled. "No you don't, you lovvve all this," then demonstrated a model's walk as she turned and laughed, then gave Deadline a hug.

He looked over Sasha's shoulder and noticed Alisha standing off to the side.

"Who's this tasty looking cup of chocolate you have with you Sasha?"

"Hello my first name is HIV; last name Virus. It's a pleasure to meet you," Alisha replied, extending her hand for Deadline to shake.

Deadline's was stunned, like he was just blinded by an up close flash from a camera.

Alisha laughed hard. "Hello Deadline, I'm Alisha. Nice to meet you."

Oh I see," Deadline smirked, "you wanna be comedian like your partner ol' crip keeper over there?"

Deadline's partners were weak with laughter from his response but his partner Bones hollered,

"Yooooo they ripped yo ass son!"

"Mannn fuck you," Deadline spat at Bones.

"C'mon chick. We got some real business to tend to instead of fuckin' with Deadline's crazy ass. Catch you later Deadline," Sasha said, shutting the conversation down as she and Alisha walked off.

"Alright homie," Deadline chuckled. "Let me know if you need me for anything. You know I'm a jack of all trades."

In the elevator on their way up to the eighth floor, Alisha uttered..

"Deadline something else girl, but he seem like cool peeps."

"He's definitely cool peeps, with his shit talking ass," Sasha laughed.

"He been trying to get at me for a good while now, but I look at him more like a brother. He always looks out for me; make sure I'm good. He a street hustler; got this neighborhood on lock with heroin and cocaine. But I don't fuck with cats that live or hang out this close to where I lay my head, feel me?"

"Girl yes, I know exactly what you mean," Alisha agreed.

The elevator finally reached Sasha's floor and they walked seven doors down the hallway til they stopped in front of Sasha's apartment, #8. When they walked in, Sasha flipped the light switch on and Alisha's mouth hit the floor. She was amazed at how decked out everything was and all she'd seen was the living room so far.

There was a 60' flat screen television mounted on the wall, a complete black suede living room set, an entertainment center, clean white carpet, beautiful black marble tables and table ends, a beautiful chandelier hanging from the wall in the middle of the living room, paintings of black art hung everywhere and beautifully sculpted black artifacts were neatly and nicely set all around the living room.

"Sheeeeiiiiit!!" Alisha exclaimed. "Girl you sure YOU ain't got the hood on lock instead of Deadline? You in Marcy living like you in Hollywood!"

"Oh no ma'am!" Sasha confirmed. "All of THIS is compliments of Club Gold. I make mad money at that club! On Friday nights, which is baller and celebrity nights, I rake in around three to four grand! It be some real big time celebrities in the club on those nights and they ass shed mad paper out if they interested in getting a little more than a lap dance from you. Catch the eye of one of them tricks and you good for the rest of the damn night. You ain't even got to dance no more that night if you don't want to; you could just mingle around with some of the ballers in the club and get your drink on free at their expense. And some of them ballers be chicks! I'm here cause being HERE allows me to stack major paper for my future plans, and since I gotta be here for now, I figure I may as well keep my shit upgraded to make it feel more like a home, you feel me?"

"Hunny I ain't even mad at cha'. This place is hard body and I see you loves you some black" Alisha laughed, pointing out the obvious.

"I sho' do…just like I loves me that nice juicy black ass of yours," she purred as she pulled her sundress up over her head and tossed it to the floor, revealing her naked body.

Alisha licked her lips and smiled, marveling at how gorgeously flawless Sasha's body was. She walked up behind Alisha, wrapped her arms around her waist and pressed her body against tightly against hers. When Alisha felt Sasha's body heat against hers, her inner thighs got moist.

"I'm going to make slow, passionate love to you," she whispered in Sasha's ear. "I'm going to bring your love down and have you cumming and moaning in deep pleasure over and over and over again."

Alisha lay her head back against Sasha's chest, letting out a soft sigh as her tongue traced invisible lines upon her neck. Sasha slowly pulled Alisha's shirt up over her head to reveal her juicy set of D-cup breasts. She rubbed her hands over Alisha's breasts, caressing them through her bra like she was molding a slab of clay, then she slowly unfastened Alisha's bra and let it fall to the floor. Her tits stood firm at attention and bounced around like they were just freed from ten years of forced bondage.

Sasha slowly eased around to the front of Alisha and began tracing the lining of her lips with her tongue before engulfing her lips with her own and diving her tongue into her mouth as they played love games with each other. As their kiss grew more intense, Sasha slowly backed Alisha up against the wall and slid her hand inside her panties to her now heated love box and began massaging its lips with two of her fingers.

Alisha couldn't believe that Sasha's touch was THIS magnificent. She'd definitely experienced sex with other women, but Sasha was very obviously different. She took her time and explored every crack and crevice of her body like a ship's captain exploring the world at sea. She was lost in pleasure and it was just getting started.

Sasha suddenly grabbed Alisha by the hand and pulled her into her bedroom. She lay Alisha flat on the bed as she climbed on top of her, kissing her from her mouth, down her chest, til she reached Alisha's love box; then she stopped to look into Alisha's eyes.

She then resumed by kissing from Alisha's stomach up to her chest and cupped one of Alisha's nipples with her mouth while sliding one of her fingers inside of Alisha love box, giving it the pleasure that it was screaming for. Sasha continued with her tongue, licking under Alisha's chin then biting softly upon her neck. Sasha slid herself down Alisha's body, took her hands and spread her legs open, revealing her golden paradise and began nibbling softly at its lips, sliding her soft wet tongue deep into its ocean.

Alisha arched her chest in the air off of the bed and ran her fingers through Sasha's hair as she released loud cries of pleasure.

When Sasha felt Alisha grip her head tight with her hands, she knew Alisha was about to explode into a world of ecstasy. She rubbed Alicia's tits and pulled harder at her nipples while greedily sucking and licking Alicia's pussy as if it would extend her own life.

Boom!

Alisha's love came down, exploding into galaxies of orgasms as she cried out, and seconds later, her body fell flat to the bed, numb but relaxed. Alisha lay there breathing heavily as Sasha rubbed her hands up and down her legs and thighs, sending chills throughout her body.

Sasha then stood up and said..

"Come on sexy. We both got to shower and prepare for a banging night out in the city. We gone be flexing hard body!"

Sasha is the only family Alisha has right now. During her incarceration, her mother was involved in a tragic car accident and was killed. Alisha became so angry she swore she'd kill the woman who prosecuted her during her case, and she stills honors that promise to this day. She had no siblings that she knew of and she'd never seen or met her biological father. The closest father figure she had and was a guy named AK, a heavy drug lord in the streets of New York.

AK introduced Alisha to hustling crack cocaine as a teen on the rough streets of Brooklyn. Alisha grind   so hard out on the block that she gained the utmost respect from AK's entire team, so he gave her leadership and authority over one of his major crack spots in one of his hottest Burroughs.

AK's army, the men that worked for him under his command, never tested Alisha because she truly was about that street life; besides, she was like a daughter to AK, and knew beefing with her would bring heavy wrath from boss man, and they knew that meant death in a strange way. Alisha happened to be inside the crack spot she held authority over the day the Feds kicked the place in and found heavy amounts of crack cocaine. She, along with numerous others were immediately arrested, charged and sentenced to serve time in prison. Alisha lucked out; she was only sentenced to five years state time for conspiracy. She vehemently refused to cop a deal with the DA to give up her supplier, so they stuck her with conspiracy; plus, one of the workers took on the drugs, and most importantly, AK had gotten her a damn good lawyer.

Sasha and Alisha both headed to the bathroom to shower after that awesome lovemaking. Alisha was grinning from ear-to-ear because she couldn't believe what had just occurred. *Oh yeah* Alisha thought to herself, *I need ALL of that ass in my life.. and I'mma make sure it stays mine...*

Chapter Six

Lorenzo decided to go to the kitchen to see what Mom Dukes had on deck in the fridge while he awaited her return. He really missed those tasty dinners his mother used to prepare for him in his younger days. She was the mother of ALL mothers. He called her the "Johnnie Cochran of the Kitchen" but to his friends, she was Momma Barnes. They loved coming over to his house to visit because she always fed them and treated them like they were her own. Even the parents in their neighborhood loved her because of the genuine love and true discipline she bestowed upon their children. Hell, even some of them addressed her as Mother Barnes.

Lorenzo walked into the kitchen and, just as he thought, dinner was on the stove, looking just as pretty and tasty as he'd always remembered. He grabbed a plate and some silverware and began digging into the pans.

One was filled with succulent beef spare-ribs smothered in a sweet-smelling honey barbecue sauce; in the pan next to it was white rice drenched in gravy; and next to that was a pan of her famous, made-from-scratch sweet cornbread that literally melted in your mouth with every single bite. The other pans were filled to the brim with macaroni and cheese, collard greens, baked beans and hot rolls, also made-from-scratch. His mother always cooked enough for Lorenzo to not only get full, but just in case company came by.

Lorenzo filled his plate with a lot of everything, poured him a giant mason jar of her lemonade sweet tea, and then took a seat at the dinner table, ready to put in work, just like old times. After devouring his meal, all he had strength left to do was slump down in his chair and smile like he was Sylvester and he'd just eaten Tweety-Bird.

When Gina Mae finally walked back into the living room and noticed Lorenzo was no longer sitting on the couch where she'd left him, she placed the photo album of pictures down on the coffee table and headed to the only other room in the house where she knew she could find him. She walked into the kitchen and found Lorenzo sinking into a near food-induced coma.

"Yep," Gina Mae laughed, "my baby boy is still the same ol' baby at the dinner table."

Lorenzo emphatically declared, "Mom you still Johnnie Cochran!" They both burst into laughter.

Lorenzo got up from the table and walked over to the sink to wash his dishes and clean up after himself.

"Hhmm…I see you also haven't forgotten your manners and lessons you were taught," Gina Mae beamed.

"How could I when I was taught by the best teacher and mother in the entire universe?" he replied.

Gina Mae's smile stretched from ear-to-ear.

"I love you son and I want the very best for you. I hope you know that."

"I know you do mom," he smiled, "and I'm going to make a great life for myself, I promise you."

"Of course you will son, cause you if don't, you already know I'll tear your behind up. Homie don't play that!"

Lorenzo laughed and gave his mother a big kiss her on the cheek.

"I love you mom. I'm going to head on up to my room and get some rest. That bus ride, plus that banger of a dinner, added laziness to me, and I was already feeling sleepy as it is."

"Okay son. I just thank God for bringing you back home to me safely. I love you."

"Nope, I love you more," he replied. He gave her another kiss on the cheek and headed upstairs to his room to get some much needed rest.

As he entered his room and cut the lights on, he was amazed at how clean and in order it still was. He smiled because it showed just how much his mother loved him and how she put in time and effort preparing for his return back home.

Tired, he wasted no time kicking his shoes off and hopping in his bed to get him some much needed shuteye, and when he did he couldn't help but continue to smile at the thought of FINALLY being back home in the soft comfort of his bed. And as he wrapped himself in the plushness of his down comforter, he knew he'd never forget the many backaches he'd suffered from sleeping on that brick of a bed while in prison.

Chapter Seven

When Alisha entered the bathroom, Sasha was already bent over the tub, setting the water temperature for their shower together. She lingered at the door for a moment, gazing at Sasha's perfectly round ass.

"I guess what they say is true," she mused.

"And what is that?" Sasha smiled, glancing over her shoulder.

"That the ass looks even prettier when it's bent over," Alisha replied.

Sasha burst into laughter.

"Girl go head on with your freaky ass."

Once the water was set to the perfect temperature, Alisha got into the shower, with Sasha quickly following behind. Alisha stood directly under the shower head, letting the water drench her entirely as Sasha stood there, immersed in her sexiness. She felt a tingle between her thighs as she became unbearably moist, so she moved body to body with Alisha and they instantly locked lips together. Alisha wrapped her arms around Sasha and began rubbing her hands all over Sasha's ass. She then backed Sasha up against the shower wall, put one off her hands between her thighs and began rubbing her clit.

Sasha gasped and whispered, "Oh yes….finger fuck me…please!"

Alisha honored her request by sliding one of her fingers inside Sasha's love cave and fingering her til she cried out in ecstasy. Alicia then got down on her knees, spread Sasha's legs apart and began her tongue assault upon Sasha's love cave.

Minutes later Sasha screamed out in overwhelming pleasure. Sasha grabbed Alisha's head, desperately trying to push it away, but Alisha's grip on her was to strong for her and her love juices came streaming down once again even stronger. Sasha screamed out again, gasping for air as her legs went weak. She felt herself falling but Alisha stood up in time to catch and hold her in her arms. Sasha lay slumped in Alisha's embrace, resting her head on her shoulder, breathing heavily until she finally regained control of herself.

When she did, Alisha took Sasha's shower sponge, soaked it with shower gel and water and began to softly wash her entire body until she was fully cleansed. Sasha then returned the favor to Alisha. They rinsed themselves off, got out and dried their bodies, then proceeded back to the bedroom to pick up where they'd left off.

Chapter Eight

Lorenzo awoke to the aroma of breakfast wafting through the air and knew his mom was in the kitchen puttin' it DOWN. He sat up, grinning extra hard, and looked over on the nightstand at the clock; it was 7:00 am.

"Mom is still the same ol' early bird," he chuckled to himself, standing up and heading to the bathroom to clean up. As he stood at the sink brushing his teeth, he looked himself over in the mirror and with a smirk said..

"Lorenzo…you back baby!"

When he got downstairs to the kitchen, his mother was just finishing up. He walked over and placed a kiss on her cheek.

"Good morning Ma!"

Gina Mae jumped, slightly startled.

"Oh! Good morning son. I didn't even hear you come in here. You know how I gets down with the get down in my palace."

Lorenzo laughed.

"Yes I do. And you funny mom, trying to use street slang like you all hip to the streets."

"You know I gots to keep up with the Jones', let y'all youngsters know I'm down, you feel me?" Gina Mae said, determined to sound "gangsta."

Lorenzo was almost on his knees in laughter.

"Gone sit down so we can eat," his mother laughed.

Lorenzo sat at the table, happier than a kid on Christmas Day. When he saw his mother set the table with three plates instead of two, he asked,

"Yo Ma…what's up with the extra plate?"

"We're having company for breakfast this morning," she replied, "someone that I would like you to meet."

Not even a minute later, a man dressed in a Nike jogging suit walked into the kitchen. He looked to be around 5' 11" and was built as if he hit the gym regularly. Though rather youthful looking, you could tell he had some age on him from the patches of gray on each of his side burns, in his hair, beard and mustache. He was very clean cut with an ol' skool type of swagger about him. It was clear to see that he'd been taking good care of himself over the years.

The man walked directly over to Lorenzo's mother and kissed her on the cheek.

"Good morning my lovely queen. Are you ready for our morning walk after breakfast?"

Gina Mae answered with a smile so bright it could've lit up the entire house.

"Good morning hunny! And you know I'm more than ready, especially with my handsome king!"

Lorenzo knew from their body language that he was special to her, and she to him. His mother didn't even have to introduce them to each other, because her "handsome king" immediately turned and introduced himself.

"I deeply apologize for my rudeness, young man. I'm Thatcher Conway," he said, offering his hand to Lorenzo to shake.

"You must be Lorenzo. Your mother has told me so many great things about her 'baby boy'."

"It's an honor to finally meet you sir," Lorenzo answered, accepting Thatcher's hand in his.

"And if my mom has her way, she'll still be calling me her 'baby boy' even when I'm fifty years old." He looked at his mother and laughed, causing her and Thatcher to laugh as well.

"You got that right!" Gina Mae agreed. "Now everyone to the table; breakfast is ready and about to be served."

Thatcher and Lorenzo both raced to the table, mouths watering as they watched Gina Mae fill their plates with fried eggs, bacon, turkey sausage patties, corned beef hash, buttered toast with homemade peach jelly and steaming hot buttered grits, with large glasses of fresh squeezed orange juice to wash it all down.

After everyone was served, including herself, she sat down at the across from them, grabbed their hands and all three bowed their heads as Lorenzo said the grace. Once the grace was said, everyone hungrily dug in to the meal places before them. It was sheer silence at the table as everyone enjoyed their breakfast, and Gina Mae couldn't help glancing at her son between bites. She was just so grateful that he was FINALLY back home, eating with family, where he belonged.

As everyone rose from the table, Thatcher offered to help clean up the kitchen while Gina Mae relaxed.

"You rest while I take care of the dishes and putting up the leftovers."

"And I'll help you," Lorenzo piped up. "I can't let you hog ALL the cool points Mr. Conway."

"Wooooow! I've got TWO handsome men fighting to clean up the kitchen?" Gina Mae giggled.

"Rest assured you've BOTH earned your cool points for today! I'm extremely blessed to have the two greatest men in my life," she said as she exited the kitchen.

While Thatcher removed all the dishes from the table, using his own cleaning rag to wipe off the table, counter tops, chairs and stove, Lorenzo filled the sink with soapy dish water and washed all the dishes Thatcher brought to him.

"I'll take care of the floor Mr. Conway. You can go on and relax," Lorenzo insisted.

"Okay," he agreed, "but please….call me Thatcher. I insist."

"Cool," Lorenzo nodded. "Oh….thank you for sending me money while I was serving time in prison," he added, "and for taking great care of my mother. You both seem to be the perfect match."

"You're most welcome," Thatcher replied. "I'll always be here for your mother; she's my queen and she deserves to be treated as such. And please know

I'm here for you as well. I just want you to get your life back on track....that's all.

"Yes sir. Thank you."

"I got a hold of some tickets to the Booker T. Washington/ Maury High School game. I think they're both 8-0. This should be a monster head to head game. Wanna go?" Thatcher asked.

"Oh yeah! That's definitely what's up!" Lorenzo grinned.

"Then it's on like popcorn," Thatcher said as he dapped up Lorenzo. And with that, turned and walked out of the kitchen.

While mopping, Lorenzo began thinking about Alisha. He wondered how things were going for her during her own transition back into society.

"Damn, I should've at least found a way to contact her before I left the bus station, so I could at least see how she was doing from time to time," Lorenzo mumbled to himself.

Done cleaning, Lorenzo decided to head back upstairs to his room to get a little more shut eye before he got out there and beat them streets with his feet. As he breezed through the living room, he noticed his mother and Thatcher cuddled up together on the couch, watching "Love Jones".

Lorenzo chuckled and in his best Method Man voice sang, "I got a love jones for your body and your skin tone…..!" Gina Mae and Thatcher burst into laughter.

"Yeah, this thing we got called love….you should get you some baby boy," Thatcher joked.

"It's just a telephone call away."

"Just make sure you don't get the dial tone son,"

Gina Mae added as both her and Thatcher burst into more laughter.

"Oh y'all got jokes huh? Let me make myself ghost," Lorenzo laughed as he headed back up the stairs.

Chapter Nine

"So what are our plans for tonight?" Alisha asked. "I wanna shut some shit DOWN."

"Well, a homegirl of mine I work with told me that Yung Money is hosting an after party at Club 360 after their show at **The Venue** tonight. You know all them big ballers are gonna be sea deep up in that piece tonight and Sasha's gonna happily let their pockets get acquainted with this nice round ass, ya heard?" she boasted.

"Naw chick," Alisha disagreed, shaking her head. "Once they make eye contact with this thick ass sitting up in this bodysuit, it's a wrap! Them hard poles hanging in their pants gonna be high-fiving this mountain of an ass as it passes by."

They burst into laughter. "I ain't even gonna lie

though, yo ass got the whole four food groups back there: Vitamin A,B,C, and D," Sasha hollered.

Alisha fell to the floor laughing, "Hell naw, you ain't say all four! Girl you got me weak!"

"You were always a slim P.Y.T. with a nice petite ass, but then you caught that bid and returned to the set with two huge bubbles on your back" Sasha drooled, eyeing Alisha's ass hard.

"We can thank that state prison cornbread for all this," Alisha laughed as she jiggled her cheeks with her hands.

"I also had me a lil piece up in that joint too. She used to rub her soft hands all over this ass during night lock down hours, then put a chick to sleep after she'd dig that lizard tongue of hers all up in this ass. Sheeeeit....I was about tell them mutha fuckas on the prison release committee I ain't going home."

Sasha burst into laughter.

"Girrrl I know she loved that wet wet cause I sure hell do."

They both just burst into laughter again.

"Alright chick....my 'do is did," Alisha announced, fluffing her freshly sewn-in weave.

"Them rats gone be sour faced when I step up in that piece tonight; might even want to bang with a chick."

"Oh no hunny, that's why I'm bringing my two number 2 pencils....so I can feed them rats some lead if they don't have no act right in them," Sasha said as she pulled out a pink plated grip 9MM automatic handgun and a black 25MM automatic handgun.

"His name is Click," she said, holding up the 9, then she held up the 25, "and her name is Clap. After he click yo ass, she's going to finish by clapping that ass. Together you can call them Team Flatline."

"You fool as fuck, you know that?" Alisha cracked up laughing, shaking her head. "But that's why you'll always my dawg. Now come on…let's hurry up and get ready so we can get this party started RIIIIIIIGHT!"

"Heeeeeeeeeell yeeeeaaaaaah!" Sasha yelled. "Operation 'Shut Some Shit Down' in full effect mode baby!"

Chapter Ten

Lorenzo woke up around noon with a hard-on that would not quit. He decided to call Angelica, the chick he met on his way home from the bus station. Fortunately, she didn't have any plans for the day and eagerly welcomed his company. That's all he needed to hear.

He jumped out of bed and headed across the hall to grab himself a shower. As he immersed himself under the pulsating water streaming from the shower massage, he began thinking about Alisha and how soft her ass felt. The more he thought about her delicious thickness, the harder he became and now his hand was wrapped around his fully erect manhood. He began to think about the bomb-ass sex he shared with Alisha and started stroking himself, harder and faster.

Then his thoughts switched to Angelica. He pictured her cute face and sexy lips, her phat ass and her mountain of a chest as if he was touching and feeling them right now. He imagined her standing in the shower with him, her soft ass cheeks pressed against his body; his love muscle erected, resting between them, feeling the warm heat emanating from them. He pushed her hair aside as he passionately kissed, sucked and nibbled all over her neck while feeling her ass slowing gyrating against him. He then placed his hands on her tits and began massaging them while pulling at her nipples with his fingertips, her mouth parted a little as she licked her lips.

Lorenzo slid one hand from her chest down her stomach and between her thighs to her clit, massaging it with the tips of his fingers. She parts her legs and he slides one finger inside of her steaming love cave, causing her to release a soft whine from the unbelievable pleasure that Lorenzo was filling her with.

As Lorenzo began placing soft kisses on Angelica's shoulders, he felt chill bumps rise up on her skin. Minutes later she bent over forward, placing her hands against the wall as the water poured over her body. She wiggled her hips back and forth then looked back at Lorenzo with a seductive look in her eyes and whispered out to him,

"You better get your pussy."

He grabbed her waist with both hands and began deep-stroking her love cave, releasing soft moans himself from the way her pussy massaged his pole with its tightness, warmth and wetness. He leaned over, chest to her back and fondled her tits while he continued stroking her. He began placing soft kisses upon her neck and back as her cries became heavier and more intense. She reached back with one arm and gripped her hand onto his thigh.

Lorenzo lifted himself back in the upright position as he continued to stroke her pussy with honor. He grabbed a hand full of her hair and carefully pulled it back until her head was looking forward, then began delivering long, massively deep strokes to her sugar walls, banging his torso hard against her backside as she cries out,

"Oh Lorenzo.. this dick belongs to me!"

Lorenzo was at the brink of exploding when he heard the sound of a lawnmower crank up, throwing his concentration completely off. He took a breath, laughed, then thought to himself, *What in the hell am I doing? I'm free now, surrounded by all this ass out here looking for some good wood. Man I'm tripping. I been gone way too long. I got to get up in some pussy....and quick...*

Lorenzo quickly finished his shower, got dressed and left the house, with nothing but thoughts of Angelica's soft ass and sweet pussy dancing through his mind...

CHAPTER ELEVEN

As the elevator reached the lobby and its doors opened, one of Sasha's neighbors, Jay Bird, was waiting to step on.

"Hello Sasha," he greeted as they both passed by.

"Hey neighbor," Sasha replied back as they continued on their way.

Once Sasha heard the elevator doors close, she said, "Giiiiirrrrrl he be fucking all these lil' skanks in the building. Got about five or six different baby mommas and something like eleven kids. He is sho nuff a breeder!" She and Alisha burst into laughter.

"Well damn Pearl," Alisha teased, referring to her friend as the neighborhood window watcher from the 80's sitcom 227, "you see and know every damn thing, don't you?"

"You damn right I do," she proudly replied. "Muthafucka's coo coo round this here part of town."

Alisha could only laugh and nod her head in total agreement.

As the ladies made their way through the parking lot, they encountered Deadline and some guy in the throes of a very heated, and seemingly very serious, argument. Two other guys were there with the dude that Deadline was arguing with, quietly awaiting their cue to jump if necessary.

Sasha wondered where Deadline's boys were; they were usually stuck to him like white on rice and the fact they weren't didn't sit right with her. She felt some shit was about to pop off and the next words out of Deadline's mouth confirmed those fears:

"Yeah, you put me on my feet, but I hustled and grinded hard to have my territory on lock. I fed these streets. I laid my OWN foundation. Ain't nobody taking NOTHING from Deadline, and if ANYBODY want beef with Deadline, they better bring an army wit' 'em cause you best BELIEVE Deadline gots one!"

"Suit yourself dawg," the guy replied. "Just remember....you HAD an army."

As they walked away, one of the other guys turned around and yelled, "I'll be to see you dawg…believe that!"

"Bring it!" Deadline hollered back. "Ain't nobody scared! We hard body round here!"

"Girl them dudes look like they wasn't playin' with his ass," Alisha said nervously as they climbed in the car. "They looked sum'um serious."

"Girl yeeeesssss!" Sasha agreed. "But they better be on they shit for real for real cause Deadline got some MAJOR juice in this hood, you hear me? His army is strong, his army is loyal and they ALWAYS ready to wreak havoc on his every call.

"Yeah I hear you but remember....I don't care who you are, money make the world go round, and when it all falls down, these nuccas ain't loyal."

Sasha started the car and pulled out of the parking lot while continuing to tell Alisha more about Deadline.

"Although he do what he do and we all know it ain't right, he does a lot of good around here too. He always be throwing functions for the kids and helps folks with their bills and even orders his goons to help all the old folk whenever they're in need, so he kind of keep shit on the up-and-up back here," Sasha explained.

"So I guess he like the ghetto Superman slash Tony Montana," Alisha said, sounding very unimpressed.

Sasha laughed.

"Nah, I wouldn't say all that, but he really IS a good dude who had no one else to turn to but the streets. His father, they call him Brick, was a local drug lord dealing major weight here in New York; he had shit on lock! But then this dude named Shyy came down from Florida with HIS peeps and set up shop on Brick's turf. Shyy and his team was hustling in the hood adjacent to us and started rising up in the game, but they was dirty bout they shit. Like if you didn't score your drugs from him, he'd have his team stomp you til you did, and if THAT didn't bring you over to his side, he'd put out a hit on you..."

"..Everybody was terrified of him and I truly believe he got NYPD on his payroll cause they don't fuck with him much. Shyy definitely got a lot of shit on lock, but MY hood bring in major paper. Shyy want control of our hood and the paper flow, but Deadline ain't bout to let that shit happen."

"Anywaaaaay….," Alisha faked yawned, "I don't care about none of that. All them ballers is waiting on us! I'm out the joint and finally back home where I belong….I'm ready to set it OFF!"

CHAPTER TWELVE

The phone rang a few times before she finally answered. "Hello?"

"Hello Angelica….this is Lorenzo."

"Well heeeyyy muscle man," she smiled into the phone. "I actually had you on my mind today."

"Thinking about a brother already, huh?" Lorenzo grinned. "That's a good sign."

"Hey, don't be getting all excited or anything," Angelica said with a slight huff. "You just crossed my mind right quick….that's all."

"Riiiiiiight….." Lorenzo chuckled.

"Anyway," she sighed, "what's your plans for today? You just got out so I know you're probably planning to hook up with some old friends and catch up, or maybe visit one of your old skeezers huh?"

Lorenzo laughed and replied, "I don't do skeezers, and I was actually calling YOU to see what YOUR plans were. Perhaps we can do lunch then maybe take a walk in the park so we can talk and get to know each other a little better. That is if it's okay with you and if all your men janks wouldn't mind."

"I don't have any men janks," Angelica laughed. "And it sounds like you're really trying to woo me, being all romantic and whatnot. You sure this ain't no game you trying to run on me? Cause I WILL kick yo ass if you fuck with my feelings."

"No game playing over here beautiful," Lorenzo promised her. "Lorenzo ain't bout that life. I just want to get to know all about Angelica."

"Well then, I'd very much enjoy going on this date with you Lorenzo," Angelica confirmed. "But don't think for one minute you gone get you some," she said immediately after.

"Get some of what?" Lorenzo asked. "I haven't the slightest idea what you're talking about young lady."

"Uumm hmm," Angelica replied with a hint of sarcasm, "what all you guys want: some sex with no strings attached. Well let me just let you know right now that I'm not about to be your first victim."

Lorenzo laughed at her sudden attitude shift.

"Hmmmm…I don't know that dude 'you guys.' He must be content with looking for a girl strictly to get his johnson wet. I'm not that guy. Lorenzo is looking for a woman to call his own; someone to love, grow and build with. And if she doesn't fit that picture then I guess that picture won't be getting painted."

Angelica smiled wide. "Well listen at you….spittin' that 'G' shit. Talk is cheap though….we'll see if you REALLY bout that life."

Lorenzo smiled. "Oh yes my darling…we certainly will.

They talked for about 10 more minutes, truly enjoying each other's conversation, and concluded with him giving her his address and confirming their date for 4pm.

Lorenzo hung up and looked up at clock on the wall; it was already 11:03. He needed to get a move on. He had to get to a bank to cash his check and do some quick shopping for some new gear to wear out on his date. He quickly grabbed his house key and ID, checked to make sure he had his check from prison in his pocket and dashed out the door.

As he briskly strolled down the sidewalk, Lorenzo couldn't help but smile; it felt so good to be home. It's hot outside and the chicks were everywhere. As he walked past them, they greeted him with stares that made him feel like he was a barbecue rib straight off the grill. He remembered the fellas in prison saying a dude coming out of prison will look different than all the other dudes on the street cause your skin will be bright and clean, your body will be looking healthy and you'll have that glow. You'll be like a walking trophy and every woman will want to claim her 'prize' before some other woman grabs it.

Lorenzo was about to cross the street when he heard someone yell out his name. He looked around to see who it was, and as the guy got closer to him, he finally realized it was his homeboy was childhood, Mario. When he reached Lorenzo, he gave him a huge brotherly hug.

"Man I ain't know you was home already Ace," Mario grinned. "Your mom told me you wasn't due to show til next month."

Lorenzo nodded. "Yeah I told her that just to surprise her."

"Yo you got swole up in that joint I see. What…they had you on the chain gang? Lifting old cars and shit?" Mario laughed. "Yeah you HAD to get swole so you could keep them punks up off that ass!"

"Man go to hell," Lorenzo chuckled, sucking his teeth. "It's not all like they say it is, but it's no place to be. You got to be mentally strong behind the walls of the devil."

"I'm just joking with you homie," Mario laughed again, throwing his hands up. "I'm glad you finally back home Ace. As you can see, ain't too much changed except some scenery and technology."

"Yeah tell me about it," Lorenzo agreed. "I see they got cellphones small enough to fit in ya pocket now. That shit is so dope I gots to cop me one."

Mario nodded. "Yeah you definitely need to get connected. You just coming home fresh out the joint and them hunnies gone be at you for a minute. You're a real hot commodity right now. Most of these dudes out here are either tore up from the floor up or they snortin' that shit. Walking round here looking like zombies and shit. Hell…some of these chicks basin' too, so be REAL careful who you fuck with cause they setting niggas up decent man."

"You ain't neva lied dawg," Lorenzo laughed. "Shit I seen this dude yesterday looking like a walking Halloween decoration. I was like damn…maybe they holding a casting call for a remake of Michael Jackson's 'Thriller' video or something."

Mario howled with laughter.

"True Ace! Welcome to Tales from the Hood: Operation Yuckmouth!"

Lorenzo almost fell to the ground, weak with laughter.

"Yo you funny as hell man! But anyway Mario, I gots to roll homie; need to handle a few things. I met this banging chick on my way home from the bus station the other day and we about to go on a date in a few so I got to grab some gear, you feel me?"

"I feel you Ace. Gone do yo thang homie," Mario said as he and Lorenzo dapped each other up. "I'll stop by ya crib tomorrow."

"Alright, homie," Lorenzo responded then continued on his way as well.

As soon as Lorenzo turned the corner he was at his neighborhood's shopping center. There were all types of stores right his disposal: Radio Shack; Family Dollar; Lucky Tan's Chinese restaurant; Athlete's Feet Shoe Store; DTLR Clothing Shop; Food Lion; T-Mobile; The Bennett's Barber and Beauty School; Chuck's Bingo Hall; and a BB&T Bank. Lorenzo headed for the bank first to cash his check.

When he got in line, there were only two people ahead of him, so fortunately he reached the teller window in no time. He requested to get his $2700 prison release check cashed, but was told he would need to open an account first in order to do so. So he opened an account with the required $100 deposit and took the remaining $2600 to handle some very necessary business with.

First, Lorenzo went next door to DTLR and quickly picked out 3 pairs of casual pants; 3 collared shirts to match them; a pair of white low-top Jordans; and 2 pairs of Polo shoes. He still needed to run over to T-Mobile to get a cellphone but seeing as it was already 2:30, he knew he'd have to save that for tomorrow, so he paid for his items and hurried home to prepare for his date with Angelica. By the time he walked back in the house, it was already 2:57; he had to get his hustle on if he was to be ready by the time Angelica showed up.

Twenty minutes later, Lorenzo was out of the shower, body fresh and clean with teeth and breath to match. He stood in the mirror brushing his hair, smiling and admiring the deep waves that were forming, and marveling at the pure lean muscle he'd packed on while in prison. He whispered to himself,

"Yeah, Lorenzo…it's time to show and prove."

He grabbed his bottle of Polo Sport cologne off the dresser and dabbed himself a few times, then he grabbed one of the DTLR bags and pulled out his new beige pants, his new beige Polo shirt with the streak of brown in it and his beige-n-brown Polo shoes.

Once dressed, Lorenzo gave himself one last glance in the mirror to ensure that he was in his best GQ status. Satisfied with the reflection staring back at him, he headed downstairs to wait for Angelica. As soon as he reached the bottom of the staircase, the phone rang.

"Hello?" Lorenzo answered, smiling.

"Hello Lorenzo….this is Angelica," she cooed into the receiver. "I'm outside muscle man; don't keep momma waiting."

He laughed. "Alright beautiful; I'm on my way out the door this very minute."

He hung up, made sure all the lights were off in the house then headed out the door, locking it behind him. As soon as he turned around to head to Angelica's car, he was literally face-to-face with her because she was standing right there in front of him.

"I see SOMEONE couldn't wait to see Mandingo," Lorenzo smirked.

Angelica burst into laughter.

"Boy please…stop being so full of yourself and give a lady a hug like a gentleman is supposed to."

Lorenzo gladly did as he was instructed, wrapping his arms around her tiny waist as he pulled her closer to him.

"Mmmm…I could definitely get used to this," she purred in his ear.

"Is that right?" Lorenzo smiled. "Well c'mon pretty lady. We'll have plenty of time to discuss that over lunch."

Angelica couldn't help but be impressed when Lorenzo walked her around to the driver side of her car and opened the door for her. He then trotted back around to the passenger side and got in. Angelica started up the car and pulled off, still smiling.

"So where are we headed first to kick off this wonderful first date of ours?" he asked.

"The Bonefish Grill," Angelica replied. "I'm telling you….you're going to love the food and service."

"Wooooow….a beautiful woman AND great food? Me love you long time!"

"Oh my," Angelica purred. "Don't start now.....you gone get yourself in trouble!" They both laughed.

She veered onto the interstate and drove until they reached the Virginia Beach Boulevard exit Eight blocks later, they pulled into The Bonefish Grill. The parking lot was packed, with folks entering and exiting the restaurant, so Lorenzo figured the food here must be on point as Angelica mentioned.

Lorenzo rubbed his hands together excitedly.

"I'm bout to tear it down up in this joint! I've been waiting many a years for this day."

Angelica laughed. "You're going to absolutely love this place. Their food is excellent."

They finally found a decent enough parking spot and headed into the restaurant. Once inside, the hostess led them to their table and their waitress,

Jennifer, took their drink orders then went to retrieve them while they mulled over their menus.

"Angelica, I would rather you order for the both of us," Lorenzo insisted. "Surprise a brother with something of your chosen taste."

"Alright then Mr. Barnes," she smiled. "I think I can make that happen."

Once Angelica had perused the menu for a minute, she placed it down on the table and glanced up at Lorenzo, smiling shyly.

"What?" Lorenzo asked, smiling back at her, slightly puzzled.

"You've safely made it to first base, which lets me know that you at least know how to swing the bat," Angelica pointed out, giggling.

Lorenzo chuckled. "Well, just call me Hank Aaron because I can hit a home run at any given time."

"Oh okay Mr. Hank Aaron," Angelica smirked, "take your eye off the ball at any given time and you SHALL strike out. "

Lorenzo laughed. "I like you. I see we're going to get along just fine."

At that moment, Jennifer returned to their table to take their lunch order. Angelica looked at Lorenzo and he nodded, confirming that he still wanted her to order for him, so she told Jennifer to bring them both the seared Tilapia with macaroni and cheese and curly fries for their sides and two bowls of clam chowder to start. Jennifer typed their orders into the business Ipad, retrieved their menus and them she'll return with their orders shortly.

Angelica took a long sip of her Arnold Palmer and folded her hands under her chin.

"So Lorenzo…tell me about you….and I want the TRUTH please and thank you. Were you some big time dope dealer? Or a murderer? And don't even lie cause you know I can find out."

Lorenzo dropped his eyes and smiled softly.

"No I didn't kill anyone…and I'm FAR from a kingpin. I am a victim of conspiracy though."

Angelica cocked her right eyebrow at him, and Lorenzo took that as his cue. He swallowed down a giant gulp of his Arnold Palmer, took a deep breath and began his story:

"My childhood friend, Marcus, robbed someone at gunpoint when we were in our early 20's. I had no knowledge of that incident, but one day we were walking through the neighborhood of Huntersville and he ran into the guy he robbed. Of course, they exchanged words, a few fists were thrown and then out of no damn where, Marcus pulls a gun out of his waist and shoots this dude three times. The guy straight drops; I mean just like that! Marcus ran, and because I was dumbfounded at what had just happened right before my eyes, I ran too. A few days later they picked us both up for questioning. There were tons of people outside that day who witnessed everything, so naturally they put us at the scene and identified Marcus as the shooter. They tried hard to get me to give him up but I refused to snitch on him, so I was charged with accessory to murder and fleeing the scene of a crime..." He took a breath...the memories still fresh and painful.

".. I was sentenced to 10 years in the Virginia State prison. It actually would've been WAY longer that that but my mom was a highly respected state prosecutor during that time and she pulled A LOT of strings on my behalf, so they were VERY lenient with my sentence. Shortly thereafter, my mom became so stressed about my situation, she retired from her career after 25 years of service."

Lorenzo sighed heavily again and looked back up at Angelica. "I really hope this doesn't change your opinion of me."

"Absolutely not!" Angelica emphatically replied as she reached across the table and placed her hands over his.

"I really like you and I hope that this is only the beginning for us. Unfortunately, we would have to keep this on the down low for now because of my job. My career would be toast if they found out I was in a relationship with a convicted felon."

"Don't you worry your pretty little head about that. I don't intend to do anything that could potentially compromise your career or us," Lorenzo assured her.

"Well, just know that I'm so happy we're here right now and I'm hoping to get to know more of you," Angelica confessed. "So far I'm very intrigued."

"Well Angelica, getting to know more of me will be totally up to you," Lorenzo smiled, staring deeply into her eyes. "I'm like a book… if you want to know the story then you must open it up and read it."

"Mmmmmm…are you flirting with me there Mr. Lorenzo?" Angelica cooed. "Because if you are, I should warn you definitely got me feeling some type of way right now."

Before Lorenzo could respond, Jennifer came walking up with their food.

"Okay here are your orders," she said, setting their plates in front of them. "Is there anything else I can get for you?"

"No Jenny, I think this will be all for us. Thank you for your warm service," Angelica smiled.

"You're so welcome," Jennifer said, returning the smile to them both. "I'll be back shortly with your check. Enjoy your meals."

Angelica snatched up her fork and prepared to dig in to her food when suddenly Lorenzo grabbed her hand.

"What?" she asked, slightly taken aback.

"We didn't say grace yet," he replied, immediately closing his eyes and launching into a brief prayer that thanked God for the food that had been placed before them and the hands that had prepared them. Angelica was stunned and, dare she admit, extremely turned on at that moment. She even said her own little silent prayer of thanks as Lorenzo was closing:

"Lord….I have NO idea what I did to deserve to hit the jackpot like this….but I thank You! We finally got us a winner!"

When Lorenzo said "Amen," Angelica opened her eyes and gushed like a giddy schoolgirl at him. "Mr. Lorenzo, Mr. Lorenzo….you are most definitely full of surprises."

He smiled and winked at her, then they both dug into their meals like there was no tomorrow, conversing about everything under the sun, the moon AND the stars. Before they knew it was 2 hours later, their plates were long since cleaned and the dinner crowd was starting to trickle in.

"I hope you're not ready for the evening to end just yet," Angelica hinted, "because I'd love if you came over to my place for a little while. We can kick back, relax….maybe watch a movie…?"

"That does sound quite relaxing…..just as long as whatever we watch movie isn't a cop movie", Lorenzo teased.

"Oh ha ha!" Angelica feigned laughter as she playfully punched him in the arm. As they gathered themselves from the table, Lorenzo left Jennifer a $10 tip and proceeded to the front of the restaurant to pay their check.

"How was everything?" the young man behind the register smiled.

"Everything was great!" Lorenzo praised. "The food was excellent and our waitress was very accommodating. We'll definitely be back."

"Awesome! I'm glad you enjoyed everything," the young man happily replied. "Well, sir, your total is $29.74. Will that be cash, credit or debit?"

Lorenzo informed the cashier that he would be paying in cash and handed him three crisp $10 dollar bills. The young man thanked them again for their patronage and told them to come back soon.

Angelica and Lorenzo promised they would walked out of the restaurant.

As they headed back to her car, Lorenzo couldn't himself as he ogled Angelica's ass, contently watching it as it bounced around inside of the dress she was wearing. He imagined rubbing it, squeezing its softness, even slipping her dress off revealing the panties that held all that ass in bondage. He imagined touching her naked body and exploring her every curve with his tongue, fantasizing about how it would taste between them thighs and sliding his love pole deep inside her sacred world, giving her deep, massive love strokes. When they reached the car, Angelica smiled back at him.

"Since I know you're wondering how soft my ass is and how it would feel in them big ol' hands of yours, if you play your cards right, all this ass will be in your hands and on your face.

Lorenzo sidled up really close behind her and nuzzled his face in her neck. "I got something else you can sit on too."

At that suggestion, Angelica reached back and grabbed Lorenzo's crotch; to her surprise his wood was hard as a rock and long as fuck.

Angelica licked her lips. "I just might have to smother him in kisses to cool him down because him seems so angry right now."

"Kisses are openly welcomed 24/7 at your own availability," Lorenzo moaned teasingly.

"I knew your horny ass was a freak," Angelica laughed.

"Yep," Lorenzo nodded. "Freak by day; super freak by night."

Once they both settled in the car, Angelica cranked it up, grabbed her mp3 player that was connected to her car stereo system, pressed a couple buttons and the sounds of Maxwell's 'This Woman's Work' bumped through the speakers. Lorenzo leaned his seat back and relaxed, allowing his mind to drift back to his 10-year incarceration and come back to the present, to the beautiful woman sitting next to him who just might give him some real good loving tonight. *I ain't had none in TOO damn long* he thought to himself. *Three long deep strokes up in that coochie and I might bust a strong nut in an instant, but you can best believe it's gone be sparks flying after that first one; that coochie gone catch some real wreck from that point on.* He chuckled at the thought.

Angelica looked over at Lorenzo and smiled, turning the music down.

"Ummm....now what are you over there cheesing all hard about buddy?"

"Oh nothing," Lorenzo said, looking over at her, "just glad to finally be free and here with you....that's all."

Angelica blushed, then turned the volume back up. Other than the music playing, the rest of the ride was in silence as they each escaped into their own private thoughts.

Minutes later, Angelica pulled up in front of her house. Lorenzo marveled at its size and how nice it looked. Her yard was clean and nicely groomed, and he also noticed a dark blue 2006 Lincoln Navigator parked in her driveway.

"Mmm hmm....look at YOU," Lorenzo nodded, beyond impressed. "You must be a drug queen pin on the low....living THIS nice at such a young age. Let me find you ridin' dirty."

Angelica laughed. "Not I baby. I have great credit; know how to save my money and spend it on worthwhile purchases; I pay my bills on time; I pray; I work hard and I always try to be a blessing to others."

"Well excuse me Ms. Superwoman," Lorenzo teased. "Allow me to just touch your cape."

"Oh you're excused hunny buns," Angelica smirked. "Now come on....we have some movies to watch and some much needed cuddling to do."

When they entered Angelica's house, Lorenzo looked around and marveled at how nice and cozy Angelica's home looked and felt. She had expensive taste, but still managed not to lose the serenity and comfort of the overall atmosphere.

"You have a very nice home Angelica, and I see you have expensive tastes too. What in the world do you want with me?" Lorenzo asked, shaking his head. "Cause I can't afford nice things like this for you right now....just being honest."

"You answered it Lorenzo...I just want honesty; I really feel you will give me that," Angelica replied.

Lorenzo took a seat on the couch and noticed many framed photos of what he guessed was her family placed around the house. There was one picture that really caught his eye; it was of Angelica at a young age with another young girl, an older woman and an older man. Lorenzo figured that to be her immediate family.

"That's my mother, father and younger sister," Angelica informed him as she handed him the glass of wine that she'd poured for him.

"The apple sure didn't fall far from the tree because your mom is a bombshell," Lorenzo whistled. "And your pops look like he could snap a man in two with his bare hands."

"Yep…so you better act like you know paht'nuh," Angelica smiled.

"Where do they live? Now that we're working towards building something, I know I'll have to meet them soon," Lorenzo mused.

Angelica looked away. "They were killed in a car accident four years ago by a drunk driver."

"Oh….I'm sorry..." Lorenzo apologized.

"..Please forgive me for asking." He set his wine glass down on the table and went over to Angelica, wrapping her in his embrace and softly rubbing her back. "

"It's fine Lorenzo," she assured him. "I went through a deep two year depression where I didn't want anyone around me…..not even the love and comfort of a good man; I felt so alone in the world.

I guess that's what drove me to become a police officer."

"Yeah, I'm actually still tripping off the fact that the first female I meet and really take a liking to is an officer of the law," Lorenzo laughed. "Maybe this is God's way of telling me He gone make sure I stay a free man."

Angelica laughed and suddenly kissed Lorenzo softly on his lips.

"I'm really glad I met you Lorenzo," she whispered softly, smiling.

"Give me just a minute to freshen up and change into something more relaxing so we can get our cuddle on and watch some movies, okay?"

"Okay," Lorenzo agreed, watching as he disappeared down her dark hallway.

He resumed his spot on the couch, grabbed the remote to the television off the living room table and turned the television on to "SportsCenter." He sank deep into the cushions and sipped on his glass of wine, eagerly awaiting Angelica's return...

Chapter Thirteen

Alisha and Sasha got in line at Club 360 and began checking out everyone that was waiting to enter the club along with them. There were definitely some major ballers, male AND female, so they knew their game had to be tight if they were going to get in any of them pockets.

"Giiiiiirirl best believe I'm coming up out this joint with SOMEBODY man and cash tonight," Alisha proclaimed. "And if not the man, then the cash will damn sure do."

"Shit I'm already locked in on my pluck for tonight," Sasha grinned.

"Who you got in your sights already?" Alisha asked. "Don't be all stingy with the info!"

"Oh hell naw trick," Sasha laughed. "I'm not about to tell you for yo sneaky ass to come and jack my bait!"

"Tru dat. There's definitely plenty more fish in that sea," Alisha bragged. "Besides, I gots me a strong rod and the best bait that money can buy.....this mountain of beef right here!" She turned around and grabbed a hand full of her ass.

"Baby you ain't never lied!" Sasha agreed, grabbing a handful of Alisha's ass and squeezing it. "Feels just like Charmin!"

They laughed and a female that was standing directly behind them inserted herself into their conversation, saying, "Yeah ma, to be honest I've been standing here admiring that ass myself; wondering how soft that motherfucker was. I mean daaaaamn!"

Alisha and Sasha both burst into giggles.

"You see all the attention and admiration that ass gets?" Sasha exclaimed. "You need to let me borrow that muthafucka for just ONE day,...I'd show you how to shut the city DOWN!"

"But on some real shit ma, yo ass sexy and thick as fuck," the chick behind them went on to say, "and your friend here is a straight dime piece too. I'd have the best of both worlds with you two between them sheets. I'm a beast with this lizard tongue." She gave them a demonstration, sticking her tongue out as far as she could.

Alisha and Sasha looked at each other in amazement; then Sasha said, "Yeah I'm going to have to get yo digits to see what that thang all about! So what's your name, Lizard Tongue?"

"My name is Candi," she replied, pulling a piece of paper out of her pocket with her number and name already on it. "I plans for moments like this ahead of time, you feel me? Call me up sometime; I promise you won't be disappointed."

Candi then looked at Alisha and said, "And you thick'ems…it's a MUST that I put my face in that ass real soon. Anything else would be uncivilized."

"Shiiiiit….if your paper, right I'll sat this ass on yo face with no hesitation," Alisha replied. "All I know is that tongue game better be on point."

Candi chuckled. "Sweetheart, I can definitely make that ass of yours shed a tear or two. You just make this meeting happen. Oh and uhhh, don't worry…..my pockets stay bulky." She blew a kiss at Alisha and winked at Sasha as they finally made it inside the club and went their own separate directions.

The vibe of Club 360 was at a fever pitch like it always is on Friday and Saturday nights. Although Sasha frequents the club quite a bit, it was Alisha's first time there and she looked like a starry-eyed kid as she drank in the atmosphere. On one side of the club was a bar so grandiose in size, it looked as though you could easily fit two small size cars inside of it.

On another side of the club, was a booth and seating area with flat screen televisions stationed in each booth. The lights in the club were florescent, with brighter lighting in some spots. The crowd was twerking, percolating and two stepping not only on the designated dance floor but in all parts of the club as the DJ mixed up some old skool jams on the turntables.

The place was packed from wall-to-wall and everyone was looking like brand new money. Females were shaking and grinding their asses out on the floor like they were trying to get pregnant tonight. Sasha and Alisha maneuvered their way through the crowd, bobbing and weaving as they headed to the bar, nodding their heads to the music. Dudes and chicks alike were trying desperately to get their attention, but they kept it moving til they finally reached the bar where they were lucky enough to find two empty seats right next to each other. They sat down and minutes later a female bartender came over to service them.

"Hello ladies I'm Jazmine," she yelled over the music, "what can I get you?"

"I'll have a Long Island Ice Tea," Alisha yelled back.

"And I'll have some Patron," yelled Sasha.

"Okay ladies I'll have your drinks right up" Jazmine replied as she turned and walked over to the drink station. She was walnut complexioned, standing around 5'5" in height with thick hips,

C-cup tits and a nice bubble ass to compliment her sexy.

She set their drinks in front of them, informing Sasha that hers was $6 and Alisha's was $7. Sasha reached under her dress to pull $20 from the mini pouch she had attached to her thigh but the guy sitting on the stool next to her quickly interrupted the transaction and told Jazmine,

"Please add these ladies to my drink tab for the remainder of the evening Jaz. Whatever they choose to wet their palates with is on me." He handed her a $50 dollar bill as a tip for herself.

Sasha and Alisha both thanked the gentleman for his generosity. He looked to be about 6' even, very nicely built from what they could tell in the low lighting and his attire was sleek and expensive. He was rocking a nice Rolex watch and a gold chain with a Jesus piece charm flooded with diamonds.

He had a laid back baller type of swag about him.

"You're welcome ladies," he smiled. "I'm Pele'."

Sasha smiled back. "Nice to meet you Pele'. I'm Sasha and this is my bestie Alisha."

"A pleasure to meet you as well Alisha," Pele' nodded as she smiled and responded in kind.

"I don't recall ever seeing you ladies here or even around the city before," he said, fishing for information. "What part of town you from? Or are you just visiting the city that never sleeps?"

"I'm Harlem bred," Alisha replied, "but my mom moved us here to Brooklyn when I was three. I literally just got back home from doing a lil bid in Virginia."

"Well, welcome home Alisha. I did a lil bid myself up in Riker's a while back and there is no greater feeling than being back on the set, living and enjoying life around friends and fam," Pele' grinned.

He then turned his attention to Sasha. "And what about you baby girl? Sitting here looking like mom's home- cooked breakfast."

Sasha burst into giggles. "Well I'm a true Brooklyn belle; been here my entire life. I'm an exotic dancer over at Club Gold. My girl just came home and we just out here enjoying ourselves and doing the damn thang!"

She and Alisha laughed and high-fived each other as they both hollered out "Heyyyy!"

Pele' laughed along with them and shook his head. He spoke with them for a few more minutes then told them he was going to go mingle around the club and see if any of his friends were there. He promised to link back up with them in a couple hours to take them to a nice spot to eat so he can get more acquainted with them, especially Sasha.

"That sounds fabulous," Sasha cooed. "I'm definitely looking forward to knowing more about you Pele'."

"Oh that won't be a problem at all," Pele' grinned, licking his lips as he disappeared into the crowd.

"Damn that man is FOINE girl!" Sasha squealed.

"And you can tell he got major paper too! Please believe I WILL find out cause he's damn sure going home with me tonight!"

"I can tell he was feeling you too Sasha," Alisha squealed back. "His game on point!"

"Yassss girl," Sasha purred as she swayed to the beat of 'Big Poppa' by the Notorious B.I.G. "That cat might just get the business tonight for real for real."

Sasha downed her drink and motioned for Jazmine to bring her another. Alisha, however, took her nice sweet time with hers. She knew Long Island Ice Tea wasn't nothing to fool around with; it'll sneak up on you and put yo ass on the floor without any kind of warning. Jazmine brought Sasha's second drink to her, a cup of Jose' this time. She leaned across the bar and, yelling a little louder this time, said,

"You girls must be new to the club; I haven't seen you here before."

"Yeah this is my first time here," Alisha replied.

"It's been a while, but I've been here a few times with a friend," added Sasha.

"Cash Money Records and Yung Money are going to be here tonight performing," Jazmine informed them.

"That's one of the main reasons we're here," Sasha grinned.

"I'm here to see my two future baby daddies: Drake and Lil Wayne!" Alisha squealed. "And Imam sling this ass all up in front of that stage when they come out."

They turned away from the bar, facing the dance floor to check out all the potential bait swimming in the club tonight.

"I haven't been here in a long while," Sasha began, "but this place STAY blazing! They have everything laid out in true club style."

"Yes hunny this spot is where it's at," Alisha agreed, "and this here chick is about to go twerk her ass out on the floor. This bar will be our meeting spot, ya heard?"

"Alright now, go on out there and make that money guhl!" Sasha giggled.

Alisha looked at Sasha and winked. "They call me rack city," then headed straight for the dance floor, shaking her ass at her every step as she vanished into the crowd.

Sasha dances so regularly at Club Gold that she was perfectly content to just hang out at the bar and chill. She crossed her legs and leaned back in her seat, sipping on her drink and observing the crowd doing their thang out on the dance floor. She was watching them so intensely, she didn't even notice the guy who had eased into the open seat next to her, nor did she hear him say anything til he leaned in closer and repeated himself.

"I said hello there beautiful. You enjoying the atmosphere here?" the guy asked again?

"Oh, I'm sorry," Sasha apologized. "I didn't even notice you there."

"No worries love. You must see something you really like out there; I hated to break your concentration," he laughed, teasing her.

"Naw," Sasha smiled, slightly embarrassed at being caught slipping. "I'm just checking out the scenery. I'm really feeling the vibe up in here."

"True indeed," the guy nodded. "I'm Nasir by the way, but mostly everybody calls me by my street name, Bones."

"Pleasure to meet you Bones. I'm Sasha," she replied, offering her hand to Bones to shake.

"Hmm, I see you're very ladylike…I like that," he smiled, accepting her hand.

Sasha looked Bones over: he was dressed like he was going to Sunday morning church service. Ain't nothing wrong with suits and all, but definitely not her cup of tea. Then he said the unthinkable:

"Hopefully we'll cross paths again sometime very soon; maybe go out on a lil date or sum'um. But right now, I gots to go link back up with wifey before she start tripping." And with that, he was gone just as quickly as was there.

Sasha mouth dropped open momentarily, then she burst into laughter at the foolishness of what had just occurred.

"The nerve of that busta ass mutha fucka," she muttered to herself as she shook her head. She downed the last of her drink and motioned to Jazmine to set her up again.

Seconds later, the DJ cut the music off and the lights over the stage snapped on. A dark skinned beauty wearing a butter-colored silk laced dress came from behind the curtains and yelled into her microphone,

"How you beautiful people doing out there toniiiiiight?" and the crowd screamed.

"My name is Lady Dee, and I'm your host for tonight's rap battle. We got two hot underground rappers coming to the stage to battle it out in the first ever one round elimination. The prize? Five thousand dollaaaaaars!" she hollered and the crowd screamed again.

AAAAAAAAnd," she continued, "I know you who else is in the house tonight, riiiiight?" Lady Dee teased as the crowd went crazy again, chanting Yung Money over and over again.

"Yeeeeaaaaaaah!" Lady Dee joined in the yelling. "Yung Money will definitely be hitting the stage later tonight and you already KNOW they gonna to set this stage ablaze!" The crowd went into another screaming frenzy.

"Alright, alright, alright," she laughed, "without further ado, this hot, underground rapper from Virginia is burning up the airwaves with his gritty bars, give it up for Priiiiiiiime!" The crowd screamed and cheered for Prime.

"And another dope underground rapper burning up the airwaves of Chi-town, give it up for Teflooooooon!" The crowd hollered, screamed and whistled in excitement. They were ready to see a battle.

Lady Dee faced the challengers and announced the rules to them:

"There will be no physical contact; just straight tongue lashing. You only have sixty seconds each so you better bring that heat! The crowd determines the winner! We did a coin flip earlier to determine who'll go first and that be you Teflon....so letssss goooo!"

DJ Radiation dropped a beat and Teflon launched into his tirade on the mic. The crowd went crazy, boosting him up to go in. When his time was up, Teflon looked at Prime smirked, "Bring it country boy; you should be honored to even be on stage with the likes of me. Play ya cards right, I can make you famous."

The crowd went crazy, with "ooooo's" and "aaaahhhhh's" and "ooohhh shit's" floating throughout the air.

"Daaaaaaaamn Prime!" DJ Radiation taunted. "He just through a major punch at you dawg! Teflon brought the blunt…you ready to light that muthafucka?"

Prime looked out into the crowd, raised the mic to his mouth, and calmly said, "Let's get high."

The crowd went ballistic as DJ Radiation dropped the beat. Prime looked Teflon straight in the eyes and ripped him to shreds with every verse. By the time Prime's sixty seconds was up, the crowd was yelling, "Prime! Prime! Prime! Prime!"

Lady Dee made her way back to the stage and yelled, "Okay let's bring it down a notch so ya'll can choose your winner! But first, let's give them both a big ass round of applause for a great battle!" The crowd made mad noise for them both.

In true Showtime at the Apollo fashion, Lady Dee went and stood behind Teflon. She held her hand over his head and said to the crowd,

"Alright y'all show your love for Teflon!" The crowd roared. Then she stood behind Prime and did the same. "Now show your love for Prime!" The crowd screamed and hollered so loud they damn near broke the sound barrier.

Lady Dee motioned her hands and arms to settle the crowd back down and when they did she announced,

"And the winner iiiiiiis…….Priiiiiiiiiiiiiime!" The crowd once went bananas as she gave Prime a check made out for five thousand dollars.

Prime accepted the check, thanked Lady Dee with a big hug, dapped up Teflon, and then faced the crowd, screaming,

"You guys made this happen! I appreciate y'all! One love fam!" He then exited the stage and disappeared into the crowd.

"We got one more surprise coming your way before Yung Money takes to the stage, but until then, gone get your drink and party on, and make DAMN sure you tip our lovely waitresses and our bartenders!" Lady Dee told the crowd before she vanished back behind the curtain.

DJ Radiation resumed the music by putting on a hot, new Juicy J track and the crowd of people went back to bouncing, grinding and twerking.

Chapter Fourteen

Angelica came back into the living room with nothing on but the towel she had wrapped around her body. Lorenzo hadn't heard her re-enter the room nor did he feel her presence; Sports Center had his undivided attention. Angelica sashayed over to the TV, politely turned it off and as she turned around to face him, she released her towel and allowed to fall into a heap on the floor. Lorenzo sat there with his mouth wide open, eyes languishing over Angelica's exquisite body.

"So the first movie we'll be watching this evening," she smile, "is the one we're about to make."

Lorenzo wasted no time reaching out and pulling her to him as she straddled him. He gently grabbed her face and began passionately kissing her, allowing his tongue to explore every corner of her mouth. She hungrily accepted his tongue and let out a soft moan. Then Lorenzo began licking, kissing and sucking all over her neck and Angelica threw her head back in sheer delight. He licked a trail from her neck down to the center of her breasts, capturing one in his mouth and sucking on its beautiful chocolate nipple.

He placed his hands on her ass as she continued to grind on his lap, causing his love muscle to become rock hard. Angelica's eyes crossed in pleasure as she felt every inch of it as it pressed against her, making her want him inside of her. She got up off his lap and dropped to her knees. She unzipped his pants revealing his hard manhood pressing strong inside of his boxers, wanting to be freed and feel her touch.

As Angelica slid Lorenzo's boxer's down, it stood straight up like a rocket ready to be launched. She was amazed at its thickness and its length. She licked her lips and smiled at Lorenzo, then began placing soft, wet kisses on its head, followed by quick flicks of her tongue around its circumference.

Lorenzo couldn't resist the moan that escaped from the back of his throat. He closed his eyes and leaned his head back on the couch and rubbed his hand back and forth through Angelica's hair. She looked up at him as she licked up and down his stiff manhood while simultaneously massaging his sack with one of her hands. Lorenzo gripped the couch pillow as she wrapped her warm lips around his manhood, taking in at least a few inches of it into her mouth at once.

"Oh shit baby," Lorenzo groaned, gasping for air, "your mouth feels so fuckin' good!"

Angelica continued her mouth assault on Lorenzo's manhood by taking in more of it with each and every stroke. Suddenly he stopped her, jumping as he quickly removed his shirt, pants and boxers. Then he pulled her up from the floor and laid her flat on the couch, locking his mouth with hers. He kissed her neck, down past her stomach, until finally he reached her sweet spot, nibbling and teasing its lips a few seconds before continuing his kisses down her body all the way to her feet.

He turned her over onto her stomach and began kissing her from the back of her neck down to her ass, where he wiggled his tongue wildly over her ass cheeks. He maneuvered one of her legs into a bent position, and then slid his tongue deep between the cheeks of her ass. Angelica's face squinted up as she momentarily lost her breath, then she released a loud, weeping moan as she reached back and gently grabbed Lorenzo's head. She tried her hardest to crawl away from him, but her mind wouldn't cooperate with her body; plus, Lorenzo's grip on her ass was too strong, so she just accepted defeat and succumbed to unadulterated pleasure he was giving her.

Finally, she couldn't take it anymore; she wanted him inside her that instant, so she somehow found enough strength to whisper,

"Fuck me Lorenzo! Please fuck me! I need to feel you inside me now!"

Lorenzo immediately sat up on his knees, grabbed Angelica by her waist and pulled her up into doggy style position. He spread her legs wide apart and pushed her back down into an arch. Lorenzo then slid one finger into her sweet spot, causing her to let out a guttural moan. Then he slid a second finger inside of her and began finger fucking her. Angelica was about to lose her mind. She writhed and ground her pussy onto his fingers, making him dig them deeper inside of her.

Lorenzo could tell she hadn't been intimate with anyone in a while, so he took his time preparing her for the grand prize he was about to bestow upon her. Angelica's panting suddenly become heavier and he knew she was about to reach her peak, so he quickly shoved his head between her legs and began sucking on the lips and clit of her love cave while slurping up all of her sweet juices. She screamed out his name in untamed ecstasy.

After she'd fully climaxed, he turned her over onto her back and kissing her passionately. His manhood was so hard he thought it was going to burst.

Lorenzo grabbed Angelica by her legs and drug her closer to him, causing her to fall flat on her back.

Then he held her legs straight up in the air and slowly eased his swollen penis inside of her. She put her hands up against his chest and let out a soft whine. From the tightness he felt upon entering her he knew she told the truth about her lack of sexual relations.

He slowly began stroking back and forth, sliding in deeper with each stroke. Angelica's pussy was so wet and warm, and the way its lips massaged his shaft with every stroke, he suddenly felt himself at the brink of exploding and BOOM.....he released every ounce of himself inside of her until he was completely empty.

Angelica's eyes rolled into the back of her head as she collapsed from the dick-lashing Lorenzo just put on her. She thought she had at least a few minutes to catch her breath, but to her shock and amazement, she felt Lorenzo's love pole becoming hard again and before she could say a word, he grabbed her arms, wrapped them around his neck, wrapped her legs around his waist, gripped her ass tight and stood up off of the bed, holding her in his arms as he did.

He carried her over to the nearest wall and pressed her body firmly pressed against it. Lorenzo started sucking all over Angelica's neck again and she reached down, slowly guiding his love shaft back inside of her welcoming cave...

Chapter Fifteen

As she lay on the couch watching 'A Low Down Dirty Shame,' Alisha heard loud moaning from the sounds of Ricardo and Sasha fucking. She shook her head as Sasha's moans grew louder and louder, almost on the verge of screeching. Daaaaamn….he must be serving that wood to Sasha's ass major or she just acting the scene out; either way she'd love to be getting some good wood herself right about now because it has been WAAAAAY too long. Suddenly Sasha's bedroom door swung open and she came flying out into the living room, fully dressed.

"I got just a call from one of the girls that work with me at the club," Sasha explained. "Something bad happened to her; she was crying and freaking out and begging me to come to her house asap so

I'm heading over there now to see what the hell is going on. I'll be back shortly."

"You want me to roll with you chic?" Alisha offered.

"Naw I'm good girl. Her baby daddy probably done put his hands on her again, being the punk that he is," Sasha said, sucking her teeth. "Besides, I got my two partners right in my purse so you just relax and enjoy your freedom home. I'll be back in a bit." Then she walked out the door, closing and locking it behind her.

Roughly forty-five minutes later, Sasha's room door flung open again; it was Ricardo, butt-ass naked going to the bathroom. About a minute or two later, he came out and to her surprise, he walked right past her and into the kitchen like she wasn't even sitting there.

As he headed back to Sasha's bedroom, bottle of Bud in hand, he proceeded to walk right past Alisha again without any kind of acknowledgement.

"Well excuse me!" Alisha spat at him. "I know your high yellow naked ass see me lying here." Ricardo turned and faced her. "Yes I did, but it's not like you never seen a dick before, right?"

"You're so right, but I haven't seen yours until now," Alisha replied as she stared at Ricardo's manhood, just hanging there like a tree trunk. She could help thinking to herself that he was damn sure working with a nice sized tool.

Ricardo smirked at her. "When you're done looking at the size of my pole, just let me know."

Alisha laughed as she rose from the sofa and went into the kitchen. She opened the refrigerator and purposely bent all the way over to grab a soda from the bottom shelf, allowing her ass to form a full moon in the air. The next thing she knew, Ricardo had come up behind her, grabbing her waist and pressing his torso against that full moon of hers. Alisha felt his manhood swelling as it pressed against her, causing a warm tingling feeling between her thighs.

She stood up and as she pulled off her t-shirt and sports bra, Ricardo caught her big, juicy breasts in his hands. He kissed and licked on her neck as he fondled her tits and pulled softly at their nipples. Alisha closed her eyes and lay her head back on his chest, enjoying the feel of his hands kneading and massaging her breasts.

Ricardo slid one of his hands inside of Alisha's panties and slowly entered a finger inside of her sweet spot. She reached back and grabbed the back of his head, pulled it down towards her face and kissed and sucked on his lips. She slowly gyrated her hips against Ricardo as he finger fucked her pussy. His sex pipe was now hard as a piece of steel pressing against Alisha's ass and that made her sweet spot throb for the attention it so desperately needed and desired.

She turned around to face him and he gripped her ass tightly, devouring her mouth with his tongue. Ricardo couldn't believe how soft Alisha's ass was as he rubbed and squeezed it; it turned him on so much that he needed to be inside of her. He undressed her until she was completely naked, then backed her up against the refrigerator, got down on his knees and spread her legs apart. He began placing soft kisses up and down the inside of Alisha's thick thighs, then on her clit, finally diving his tongue deep inside of her. Alisha moaned loudly as she rubbed her hands all over Ricardo's head. Her legs were shaking so much she thought they'd soon give out from under her. Ricardo felt her weakening, so he stood, picking Alisha up in his arms as he did. She wrapped her arms around his neck and her legs around his waist as he held her up by her ass. Then she reached down, grabbed his swollen shaft and placed it at the entrance of her sweet spot. Ricardo slowly slid her down onto his shaft as he entered her hot box.

Alisha threw her head back and feverishly whispered, "Oh yeeeesssss! Please go deep! I need to feel you all the way inside of me so bad!"

Ricardo felt the tightness as he slowly worked inside of her. Finally she opened up to him and he began bouncing her up and down on his hard shaft. With every thrust he delivered to her, Alisha squealed in pure delight. She felt him hitting places that hadn't been touched in far too long and soon she began showering her juices upon his shaft, triggering soft moans from his mouth. Ricardo power continued to pound her until he reached his own peak, letting out an "oh fuck" as he came.

Alisha pushed herself out of his hold, dropped down to her knees and captured half of his shaft in her mouth, sucking and massaging it with her lips until he had spread his whole load into her mouth, and she happily swallowed every drop of it. She massaged his shaft until he somehow found the strength to stop her. She kissed the head of his shaft and stood up and to her surprise, Sasha was standing there, contently watching their live action porno.

They hadn't even considered the fact that she could walk in at any moment and apparently they were so deep into fucking each other, they didn't even hear her come in. Alisha and Ricardo just stood there, wide eyed and quiet, staring at her and hoping no shit was about to pop off.

Finally, Alisha giggled and said, "Damn, chick. How long you been standing there and why yo ass ain't join the fuck in?"

"Long enough to know y'all asses didn't even know I was standing here all this damn time," Sasha laughed. "But don't worry. Ain't nobody putting no clothes back on, because Sasha is about to get out of hers and we about to take this shit to the room and make us a movie! So Ricardo," she smiled, "you better put that wood in overdrive!"

****

Hours later Alisha awakened. She looked to her right and there lay Sasha, butt naked, sleeping like a baby. She smiled to herself as she rose from the bed and walked over to the nightstand to look at the clock.

"Damn, it's 8 am," she yawned. "Guess I'll get my ass up and see what this day brings me."

Alisha walked over to her dresser and pulled out some fresh underwear.

"Mmmm....come on back over here and let momma smack that ass some more," Sasha teased in her scratchy but sexy morning voice.

Alisha turned around looked at Sasha. "Girl, I thought yo ass was sleep. You ain't get enough of smacking this ass last night? Got my ass cheeks tender as hell right now," she laughed. "I'm about to hop in the shower. What time did Ricardo leave out?"

"Girl I don't even know. That dick put a chick in a deep sleep," Sasha giggled. "That nigga got magic in that pole; some of that ol' abracadabra put a bitch to sleep type of potion."

Alisha burst into laughter. "I know that's right! That fucka had his tongue so deep in my ass I swear I felt it licking my collarbone!"

"Girl you silly as hell," Sasha said, howling with laughter. She stretched real long and hard and let out a deep sigh. "Well, let me get my ass up, too. I'mma whip us up some breakfast while you shower."

"Word, cause I could eat a whole horse right now," Alisha laughed.

"And while we're eating we're going to have us a little girl chat," Sasha demanded, "because I want all the 411 about that guy you said you met."

Alisha giggled. "Tru dat."

****

As Alisha was lotioning up and putting on her underwear, Sasha walked back into the room.

"The hell with cooking," she declared, "let's go out for IHOP….my treat."

"Shit, I'm definitely down," Alisha happily agreed.

"Word! Let me shower and put some clothes on and I'll be ready to rock," she replied.

Chapter 16

As Sasha and Alisha exited the apartment building they ran into Deadline.

"Greetings my black Nubian queens! Y'all looking all magically delicious today and as always," he grinned. "Alisha, that sitting muscle is looking quite healthy today. Mind if I be its personal trainer? I promise to give that ass a good sweat."

They both burst into laughter.

"Deadline please," Alisha huffed. "All this ass would devour you, boy."

"C'mon baby," Deadline begged. "Let me get a feel, a bite, shit let a pimp just nibble on that muthafucka or sum'um!"

As Alisha rolled her eyes at Deadline, one of his boys said to Sasha, "Hey Sasha. You looking right sexy today as you always do. I've had my eye on your fine ass for a minute now, but when the time is right, and opportunity properly presents itself, I'mma get at you on some real grown man shit cause you a bonafied cutie. Oh and by the way, I'm Reggae." He lifted her right to his lips and kissed it.

"Ooooo….thank you for the compliment Reggae," Sasha cooed. "We'll definitely see about that. Deadline…..you better take notes from him; he could help you get some real cootchie instead of tricking with them skeezers."

Deadline's crew cracked up laughing.

"Code 27, code 27…." Reggae said into his cupped hands as he pretended to be speaking into a CB radio, "Operation Get Deadline Some Classy Cootchie is now activated!" Everybody burst into laughter, including Deadline.

Y'all ain't shit!" he said through his laughter. "But I need to holla' at you on some real shit,"

Deadline said to Sasha. They walked off to the side so they could speak privately.

"I saw y'all come home the other night with ol' boy. I know that cat from somewhere and it ain't nowhere good. Just be careful ma," Deadline advised.

"Thanks for being concerned about me, but you're wrong about him," Sasha assured him. "He a good dude."

"Fuh sho. You fam and I got mad love for you Sis. You ever need me for anything, I got you; don't ever forget that," he told her with such heartfelt sincerity, Sasha almost teared up.

"Wow….thank you. I really do appreciate that. And you already know I ain't got nothing but love for your crazy ass too Deadline," she smiled at him.

In the car on the way to IHOP, Alisha told Sasha all about Lorenzo, including all the juicy details about their short sex fling at the bus station.

"Girl, the wood that cat served me with almost had me ready to say fuck New York, I'mma make my bed in Virginia!" Alisha shouted as they both laughed.

"So do you plan on contacting him or was it just a one and done thing?" Sasha asked.

"I'm hoping it's not," Alisha admitted. "I'd like to keep him around as a friend, you know, to have someone to go visit when I want a break from home and to get my back broken at the same time."

"Girl you so damn nasty," Sasha said, bursting into laughter, "but I damn sure feel you on that. Shit, I need to get ME an out-of-state wood connect!"

Alisha laughed and high-fived Sasha. "I got a letter that he dropped at the bus station with his mother's address on it, so I'm going to kick back and write him a letter. Hopefully he'll contact me from there. Do you mind if I give him your number so he can call me, at least until I have a phone of my own?"

"Sure, you know I don't mind it at all," Sasha smiled. "You know you my right hand. We gots to look out for each other. And if things jump off serious with y'all, maybe he can put me in deep with one of his homies. Birds of a feather flock together so you know his homies gonna have good wood too, but they ass better have some paper with that wood," she stated seriously, "you know Sasha ain't having that broke shit."

"I feel you on that shit girl," Alisha agreed.

They finally made it to the IHOP and upon entering, they were immediately greeted by the hostess, who seated them in one of the only available booths in the restaurant. The waitress met them at their seats, gave them menus and took their drink orders, and told them she'd return shortly to take their food orders.

"So what's the 411 on Ricardo?" Alisha asked when their waitress walked away. "What he got going on?"

"Well, I found out that he is a MAJOR drug lord in this part of town; a general as a matter of fact. I was shocked when he told me that Shyy was one of his top soldiers, which means HE is Shyy's BOSS."

"So you mean to tell me that the guys Deadline are beefing with all work under his command?" Alisha asked, sounding very surprised.

"Yes ma'am," Sasha confirmed, "and Ricardo gots MAJOR weight spread out in these streets. He got hot spots in Manhattan, Long Island AND Harlem on lock. He gots that paper and told me he's going to make sure we good cause he like how we carry ourselves and stay dolo just with each other, and if we ever need anything handled, ANYTHING, to just let him know and it WILL be handled.

"Shit, I'm definitely down with that," Alisha grinned, high-fiving Sasha.

At that moment, their waitress returned with their drinks and took their food orders. She collected their menus and promised to return with their meals shortly.

When she came back with their food, Alisha and Sasha dove into their plates like it was their last meals on earth, Alisha especially. She couldn't remember the last time she'd enjoyed a loaded chicken omelet with cheese grits and pancakes on the side. She wouldn't wish the garbage that she ate during her stint in prison on even her worst enemy.

She savagely devoured every last morsel and

when her plate was nothing short of licked clean, all she could do was lean back in the booth and smile.

"I take it you enjoyed that shit?" Sasha laughed at her friend.

"Giiiiiirrrl, I damn sure feel like I'm home now!" Alisha grinned.

"That's what's up!" Sasha replied, returning the grin. "Well, I don't know about you, but I am stuffed and I don't have the strength to do shit right now. I'm ready for a nap after this here!"

"You ain't said nothing but a word," Alisha agreed.

Sasha grabbed their check off the table, left their waitress a $10 dollar tip, paid their tab and hightailed it on back in the direction of home.

When they pulled back into the complex, they were met with complete chaos. The parking lot was packed with police cars, ambulances, the "meat wagon," which is what they call the coroner's van, hauling off a dead body and numerous police investigators questioning people that were standing around being nosy.

"Well damn!" Alisha exclaimed. "What the hell happened out here THAT damn fast and so early in the damn day? It seems like we just left!"

"Chile you know how it is in the hood….sun-up or sun-down, shit is always poppin' off." Sasha chuckled sadly, shaking her head. "But I got a really bad feeling about this scene here."

Sasha whipped her car into the first available parking space and she and Alisha jumped out, trying to push through the crowd of neighborhood folk, but before they could make it inside the building, a female officer cut them off.

"Hold up ladies! You can't go in there. You're going to have to wait until we clear the crime scene before you can go back in."

"What happened out here?" Sasha asked. "Who was killed?"

"Deadline," an elderly lady called out as she walked towards them. "Someone shot him in the head. He's dead..."

Chapter 17

Both Sasha and Alisha gasped in shock.

"Oh my God nooooo!" Sasha wailed. "Where were his boys? They weren't out here with him?"

"No, he was alone this time. He usually be with them other fellas, but not today," the older lady replied, shaking her head.

"This is so sad. He was so mannerable. He would always help me to my car and help me unload my groceries when I would get back from the store. I don't know what our young folk doing with themselves nowadays but killing one another. I feel sorry for his parents losing their baby."

Then a middle-aged gentleman standing behind Alisha chimed in.

"It's sad…we lose them so young today. But when you live by the sword, that same sword can bring you death."

Alisha and Sasha watched as they wheeled Deadline's body, already encased in a body bag, into the coroner's truck. They were sure that those same guys from earlier played a major part, if not the WHOLE part, in Deadline's death, and before long, the streets will be talking, names will be mentioned and his boys will be on the hunt for those responsible.

Finally, after what seemed like hours, the police removed the yellow tape from the building entrance and allowed everyone back inside; but detectives detained some of the neighbors for questioning, hoping to get some leads on the case.

When Alisha and Sasha got back inside Sasha's apartment, they flopped down on the couch and sat quietly for a few minutes, each lost in their own thoughts about the tragedy that just unfolded.

Finally, Sasha let out a deep sigh.

"Damn girl....we JUST joked around with Deadline this morning. Just this morning! And now he's dead! I'm telling you....something fishy is definitely going on."

"Hell yeah it is," Alisha nodded in agreement, "especially now all of a sudden his boys are nowhere to be found. This shit about to get ugly."

"Well, I need to be getting on up outta here..." Sasha said, rising from the couch.

"...I got some errands to run with one of the girls from the club. We're working together to hopefully start our own business in the very near future. I'm taking my work clothes with me so I'll just see you later on tonight."

With that, Sasha retreated to her room to pack her work clothes. She grabbed her duffel bag and threw in all her necessities for the evening, including her nine millimeter handgun that she leaves hidden in her car while she's working, then she started getting dressed.

Out in the living room, Alisha continued to lounge on the couch, allowing her mind to drift back to the scene of Deadline's murder. Then Lorenzo crossed her mind, so she got up, grabbed some paper and a pen and sat back down to begin writing her letter to him.

About 30 minutes later, Sasha came out of her room dressed in a half-white shirt that exposed her flat stomach and diamond belly ring, a gold thigh length mini skirt and a pair of gold heels. Her ass looked like brand new money.

"Well chick I'm about to beat these streets," Sasha said.

"I'll have a phone for you when I come home tonight. I left my number and some cash by the house phone just in case.

And tomorrow morning we're going to get you down to the DMV so you can get your real I.D. and get rid of that state bullshit. I think the only reason they let you in the club last night was cause you was looking all delicious with all that ass you got back there. Shit I would've too, but you would've had to let me cop a feel first."

Alisha burst out into laughter.

"Girl bye..... with your crazy ass. And you better hurt 'em tonight too. Soon as we get this ID thing straightened out, I'll be coming up to the club with you."

"Fuh sho," Sasha replied. "See ya tonight," then she walked out the door.

By the time Alisha looked back up from her now completed letter to Lorenzo, an hour had passed. She looked over at the clock; it was two o' clock in the afternoon. She got up, slipped her sneakers back on, grabbed her key and the $400 dollars that Sasha had left for her and left out the door, headed to the post office.

CHAPTER EIGHTEEN

Relaxing back on the bed, Lorenzo and Angelica laid snacking on the sandwiches she made, each cut into four squares with a bowl of Cool Ranch Doritos Chips. They watched the movie "Limitless" starring Bruce Willis. They looked at each other from time to time just smiling.

"If I could know what your ass was thinking before you even spoke your ass would be in some serious trouble there mister, " Angelica stated.

"Then you'd know how happy and grateful that I am just to be lying next to this beautiful woman who clearly ignites my wick ", Lorenzo implied.

Angelica whispered, "awww baby," grabbed their empty plate and bowl, took it to the kitchen and placed them into the dishwasher. She walked back into the room, crawling into bed to snuggle up next to Lorenzo. Wrapping one of her legs around his body and resting her head on his chest, she spoke softly.

"You really know how to make a woman feel good inside and I'm so happy I'm her. "

Lorenzo lifted his head and placed a soft kiss on her forehead before replying,
"It's my job to do so beautiful... "

They just laid there cuddled up together as they drifted off to sleep while the movie continued to play.

Hours later, Angelica was awakened by the ringing of her house phone, so she got up to go answer it.

"Hello " Angelica voice was raspy and full of sleep.

"Hey love bug! Damn, you sound like he put your ass in a deep sleep..don't let me find out that prison pipe manhandled that ass "

Dion Wallace, one of her work mates and close friends uttered out to her.

"Girl yo ass so damn nosy! You in the wrong profession.. you should a been a private investigator with your snooping ass. I'll see you at work girl" responded Angelica as she then giggled and hung the phone up.

Angelica went and climbed back into bed with Lorenzo. As she did, he awakened and muttered.

"Good morning tiger.. how's my lil love bug feeling?"

"I'm feeling like new money ", Angelica answered.

Angelica then slid her body down between Lorenzo's legs and wrapped her warm mouth around the head of Lorenzo's shaft, slowly taking his full length into her mouth as began massaged his shaft with authority.

"Oh baby, damn ", Lorenzo mumbled then moaned loudly while wildly running his fingers through Angelica's hair.

She massaged his shaft intensely until Lorenzo's dick swelled and released its entire load inside of her mouth as she swallowed every single drop. Angelica then got up went into the bathroom and hopped into the shower. Lorenzo laid there stunned, mind on blank. Just released from prison, he never imagined all of this happening for him and so soon, but he was loving every minute of it, along with Angelica.

Out of the shower and getting dressed Angelica looked at the time, it was 7:00 am, she still had an hour before she had to be at work.

"Baby, you want me to make a quick breakfast for you before we leave out", Angelica asked Lorenzo?

"No thank you baby... I'm a see what mom whipped up this morning when I get to the house I'm pretty sure she made plenty, plus I know she gone fuss me out for not calling her to let her know I'm okay being that I just got out. She's going to be like that for a while until a little time passes by and I'm doing good, I'm still her baby in her eyes ", responded Lorenzo.

"Well hopefully I get to meet mom soon before I kidnap her baby again, cause next time you're spending a little more time with me and I need her to know me as a person and as a woman, so she'll know her baby's in the best of hands. It's the respectable thing to do I think", stated Angelica.

"Oh trust me you will, she'll force me to, but you better be ready because you already know she's a retired prosecutor and her questions will be straight forward and firm.. mom don't play ", advised Lorenzo.

Angelica replied,

"What!, I'm not worried one bit.. me and your mother will get along just fine trust me. Plus, I will get the opportunity to learn so much about her past career field... okay I'm ready now. Get your behind up and get dressed before I become weak and call out of work. I'd rather be snuggled up with you the rest of the day. "

"Dang, I hate to even move, I'm so comfortable, but I do need to go home though ", Lorenzo uttered.

In the car, as Angelica drove him home, he looked over at Angelica and she had this enormous smile on her face.

Lorenzo asked, "what in the world you cheesing so hard for over there cutie?"

"Don't worry why, you just worry when I'm not cause then you have problems mister", answered Angelica.

Lorenzo laughed then went on to say, "Umm hmm, there's no such pain as that of a woman scorned. Oh yes, I've heard that before from mom's plenty of times during my life."

"Then you study and memorize that shit like it determines the passing or failing of a history test my brother, and your mother is a wise, wise woman...you better internalize her wisdom because it could teach you how to be one up on women if you pay attention when class is in session ", Angelica urged Lorenzo.

Lorenzo just smiled, knowing he was sitting in the presence of a real woman, the kind that him and his cellmate Z-man use to talk about everyday when he was serving time. He can't wait to sit down and write Z-man a letter to tell him all about Angelica and his fling with Alisha. He was sure Z-man would be waiting to hear from him.

Angelica pulled up in front of Lorenzo's house and turned the car off.

"Thank you for all of this joy and happiness that I'm feeling right now. I'm so hoping we really get to know each other much more outside of the unbelievable lovemaking we have with each other ", Angelica told Lorenzo.

"Like a running back, I'm trying to carry the ball all the way to the end zone ", Lorenzo babbled on.

"Now what in the hell has that got to do with anything I've just said" Angelica asked then laughed.

Lorenzo laughed as well.

"I haven't the slightest idea, but I just felt like saying that..."

"Look baby, tomorrow I would like to introduce you to my mother. I know she's going to love you and with you being a officer of the law, well, let's just say, you've already got one foot in the door ", Lorenzo added.

"Okay baby, anything for my Mandingo " Angelica teased then smiled at Lorenzo.

He smiled then leaned over and kissed Angelica on her lips and whispered,

"Later baby ", then exited the car.

While she watched Lorenzo walk up to his front door, she rolled down her driver's side window and yelled,

"I miss you already Lorenzo Barnes."

"Baby get your pretty self to work before I citizen's arrest you for being so damn lovable ", Lorenzo replied.

Angelica laughed then rolled the window back up and drove off. Gina Mae Barnes opened up her door and hollered out,

"There's my baby boy" then lightly smacked him upside his head when he got within reach.

"You had me so worried, didn't even call your mother to let her know that you were okay. I ought to get my belt and tare into that hiney ", added Gina Mae.

Lorenzo answered "hey ma, I love you too... "

Gina Mae left the front door open and muttered to Lorenzo.

"Ma nothing, I don't want to hear that... "

"I'm a grown man now ma, and you don't have to worry about me out there getting into trouble, trust me on that " Lorenzo told his mother.

"Yes, you are a man now, but you still my baby and only child. People are really crazy out here nowadays..." Lorenzo's mother lectured.

".. And who was that young lady in the car you just got out off that sped off so quickly? Why am I not being introduced to her?"

"Don't worry ma, you will meet her tomorrow. She asked to be introduced to you because she felt it was the respectable thing to do" Lorenzo replied.

He took one good look at his mother then blurted out.

"Oh no ma, where are you going dressed like you about to shut the city down!"

"Well, she sounds like she may be a nice young lady if she wants to meet your mother.." responded Gina Mae.

"..And, my hunnie buns and I are going out to eat, then over his daughter's house for a while, and from there to the Earth, Wind, and Fire concert. One day every week we go out on a date whether it's to a concert, show, dinner, movie, or just a walk in the park..you kids have lost the true values of life and love.. " She admonished Lorenzo.

"Depressed, worried and so alone was all I felt while you were in prison until I met Thatcher, he comforted me with respect, loyalty, protection, trust, but most of all love and continues to do so. He's an awesome man to your mother son, and he's very fond of you" Gina Mae explained.

"Ma, any man you have in you life, I know has to be extra special, being that you were with dad till his last day. Plus you ain't nobody to play with.. I know he's on point because you'll have it no other way.." Lorenzo told his mother with a smile.

"I see you know your mother quite well, but I better see that young lady tomorrow.. I'm not playing about that!" The look on her face left no questions in Lorenzo's mind.

"You will ma.. don't worry you will" Lorenzo assured her.

Gina Mae then hugged Lorenzo and whispered.

"I love you son...more than anything in this world."

"I love you more ma ", Lorenzo replied.

Then a deep voice came in through the screen door.

"Hey, who's that man my queen has her arms wrapped around? "

Lorenzo turned and looked at the screen door to see who it was. Gina Mae already knew..she knows her man's voice the instant she hears it.

Smiling, Lorenzo's mother responded.

"Hello dear" as Thatcher made his way into the house.

Thatcher kissed her on cheek then looked her over and shouted.

"Look at you looking fireplace hot! I'm beyond the luckiest man alive."

Gina Mae smiled her prettiest and blushed just enough.

"Thank you sweetie and yes, you are right, you're the luckiest man alive I must say."

Gina Mae, hair done up in an old school bun, was wearing a half white/half black knee length fitted dress, low cut neckline and her shape made the dress that much more appealing. A slick pair of all white quarter inch heels with a nice black suede handbag completed her ensemble. Her earrings were diamond studs, matching perfectly the beautiful diamond necklace she wore; all of which were gift from Thatcher.

Thatcher was dressed in an all beige Armani suit, white tipped button down dress shirt with a beige tie, beige old school hard bottom Gator dress shoes and an all beige Kangol hat. He was as clean as a new marble floor.

Thatcher said to Lorenzo.

"Hello there Lorenzo, how's everything going there young man."

"All is well on my end Sir, but I see you casket sharp...yeah you big pimpin' for sho', Lorenzo replied.

"Mom, I know it's none of my business but you two are as close as a perfect couple can get, so why aren't y'all living together under one roof" Lorenzo asked.

Thatcher blurted out.

"With all due respect, I'd like to answer that hunnie..." Thatcher spoke to Gina Mae but his eyes remained on Lorenzo. He didn't wait for permission.

"..When me and your mother first met then began dating, and our dating turned into a relationship, she made it quite clear that she didn't want to be under one roof with any man until her son was back home and her heart could be at peace again. So I stood and continue to stand by my queen until that day" Thatcher added.

Lorenzo nodded his understanding then replied.

"I can't wait..then maybe she won't worry about me as much.." Then laughed.

"Don't make me pluck you up side your head again and put you on punishment. You won't be seeing your little friend for a while" Gina Mae told Lorenzo then burst out laughing.

"Well, lets go hunnie. I'm ready to go out to eat at our favorite spot then stop over your daughter's house and spend a little time with her. I gotta get my groove on!"

Gina Mae popped her fingers, jingling her hips as they walked out the door in route to their day of festivities. Lorenzo laughed at his Mom's antics while heading into the kitchen to see if his mom cooked breakfast; she did and she left his plate in the microwave.

When finished eating, Lorenzo cleaned his dishes and wiped the table off then walked into the living room, turned the television on and just sat back, watching some shows for a while.

I'll write homie Z-man a letter tomorrow and put him down with all the scoop that's been happening with me since I've been home Lorenzo thought to himself.

Lorenzo was still a little tired and went to lay back on the sofa, but remembered that his mother didn't play about sleeping on her furniture, so he turned the television off and headed up stairs to his room to take a nap.

Chapter Nineteen

Letter to Lorenzo in the mail and now relaxing on the couch, Alisha knew it was going to take some time to get her life back on track. The thought of getting her hands on the prosecutor who'd sent her away to prison those years when she lost her mother in that fatal car accident was a major hindrance for her. She'd sworn if the opportunity ever presented itself, she'd kill the bitch and she was still standing by her word.

Remembering Sasha had fixed up the spare room for her, Alisha got up to go take her things out of Sasha's room, placing them in her own. She really appreciated Sasha and their tight friendship. With her clothes in hand, Alisha opened the door to her room and was immediately in awe of how nice and cozy Sasha had made it for her. It was fully furnished and super clean. Alisha hung her things in the closet then refolded her undergarments, putting them in one of the dresser drawers. She went back into Sasha's room for her shoes, returned to her room, placing each pair neatly on the closet floor. After arranging everything to her satisfaction, she headed back to the living room to watch some television, flicking through channels until she came upon the Jerry Springer Show. She decided to kick back and watch the antics on the show.

After Jerry Springer and a few more sitcoms, Alisha grew tired of watching television and decided to take a walk around the neighborhood to get some air and hopefully run into a few old partners from back in the day.

As the elevator door opened and she stepped out, she saw Ricardo across the street talking to two of the guys from Deadline's crew; she wondered what they were talking about. Especially Ricardo Alisha thought to herself it's strange that Deadline's boy's show their face now, but was nowhere to be found when Deadline was killed. I got to inform Sasha about this...we need to investigate this shit; something just ain't smelling right.

Alisha went on about her way, walking a few blocks to the Waverly Mini-mart to grab something to drink. The cashier had his eyes on Alisha's ass the entire time she was in the store and shook his head at how phat her ass was as she exited the store.

She continued her strolled down the sidewalk, checking out the stores and businesses she passed as she thought about her future and what she planned on doing with her life. She knew it would take some time; she'd just take each day one step at a time, right now she was simply enjoying her freedom.

"Um.. um.. um.. hey sexy. They say crack kills but I'd die by that crack any day."

This guy standing in front of a Chinese joint yelled out to Alisha as she passed by him.

Alisha just shook her head and kept walking until she came upon a shop that carried women's clothing and decided to go in to check out the merchandise. As she entered the store, she was greeted by staff.

"Hello, welcome to "The Ladies Boutique! If you need help with anything, just let me know and I'll be more than glad to be of assistance to you.."
The clerk was a nice looking young black female that seemed happy and eager to help.

"Thank you! I'll let you know if I need any assistance " Alisha replied.

Alisha took a walk around the boutique, stopping at several different clothing racks. She wasn't really planning on purchasing anything yet, just seeing what the store carried for future shopping sprees. However, she did see some things she liked and planned a return trip to the boutique soon.

Alisha exited the boutique with a wave and a promise to return and headed back to Sasha's apartment. Once again, that body of hers attracted major attention! Guys were trying to spit so many lines at her, she swore she'd heard them all. Yet, the one female that hit on her, Alisha thought was sexy as a mutha. She had that Aaliyah type look and swag; that good girl/bad girl look, but Alisha didn't have time to play right now. She had other plans she hope soon would come to fruition.

As the apartment came back into view, Alisha noticed a female standing in front by the entrance. She wondered who she was and if she was just one of the tenants in the building.

"Hello"

Alisha greeted her as she passed on her way into the building. The girl just looked at her with a sad look then put her head down. Alisha wondered to herself what was wrong with her. Maybe she just has a lot going on in her life.

As Alisha entered the apartment, locking the door behind her, she immediately went into her room, kicked off her shoes and laid back on the bed; she just wanted to relax.

Hours passed as Alisha lay in a deep sleep. When she woke, looking at the clock on the wall, it read 7:07 pm. Where in the world is Sasha she questioned silently. She was surprised she'd slept so long, but figured her body knew it needed the rest more than she did.

She got up, rinsed her face, brushed her teeth, and headed straight for the kitchen to find something to eat, her stomach feeling like it was on empty. She opened the freezer, grabbed a t.v. dinner and a bottled water out of the fridge. While waiting for her t.v. dinner in the microwave, she relaxed against the kitchen counter, her mind flashing on Lorenzo. Hope he gets my letter and won't be mad I used his mother's address...

Alisha also hoped her letter would make Lorenzo smile and have him calling Sasha's phone in no time. Oh how I would love another round with him, she thought, this time with no worries of being caught in a public place. Behind closed doors with no worries or interruptions, I'd fuck and suck the living breath out of him! She smiled, squirming just from the thought.

The microwave stopped, Alisha got her food, placed it on a plate then made a b-line to the living room. She sat eating and watching movies til her tray was empty and all the good movies were finished, so she stretched out on the couch wrapped in a blanket, enjoying "Good Times." The show reminded her of her mother, how she struggled but maintained to keep a roof over their heads and food on the table.

Alisha eyes began to water thinking about her Mom. It was so hard for her; losing her mother while she was in prison. She had bottled up so much pain, anger and hatred inside, sometimes even blaming herself. She'd tried talking to a counselor about all the pent up anger, but over time, stopped talking to the counselor about it yet somehow found the strength to make it through. Alisha sat up on the couch and as she did Sasha walked through the door.

"Damn thirsty mutha fucka! Oh hey girl" Sasha blurted to Alisha.

"Hey, what you coming through the door talkin shit bout?" Alisha asked

"Chic, these thirsty ass niggas got no chill with them... talking bout wassup ma, let me take you out sometime..shower you like a man suppose to. I'm like, how the fuck we gone go out cause yo ass walking? What the fuck we gone do, ride a two seated ten speed bike or sum'um? These niggas unreal" Sasha replied testily then broke out in squeals of laughter.

Alisha burst into laughter as well and said,

"Girl niggas just looking to get a quick shot of coochie and them broke niggas be the worst."

"Oh yeah... Chic, I got some deep shit to fill you in on... you're gonna want to investigate this shit here" Alisha added.

"Okay girl, let me put these bags over here on the table and sit my ass down so you can fill me in on what's going on" Sasha replied with rushed excitement. The look on er girl's face let her know this was some deep shit.

After placing the bags on the table, Sasha handed Alisha a bag from T-mobile. Alisha opened pulled out a cell phone with a protective case in her favorite color and design. The phone was already activated with blue-tooth. Alisha hugged Sasha, thanked her then went on to tell her about who she had seen today and who that he was talking with.

"Girl, I went out to today to take my letter to the post office to have it mailed overnight and as I come out of the apartment building, I see Ricardo, and who was he talking to? None other than Deadline's crew or homies...whatever you want to call them nothing ass niggas" Alisha explained.

"Well what did Ricardo say when he saw you? I know he spoke, the way you threw that ass back on him the other night...he better had" inquired Sasha.

"Chic, them niggas was in such deep convo, they didn't even notice my ass, but girl I smell a rat cause all of a sudden Deadline's crew show face after he was killed.. and on top of that, they in deep conversation with Ricardo. You know that nigga a drug lord out on these streets, in these hoods, what interest would he have in them nobody niggas"Alisha explained.

"Whaaaat! Since you brought it like that... now that is some deep shit. I gots to get to the bottom of this and believe me I will. Them niggas might just be on Ricardo's payroll" Sasha reasoned.

"Ricardo called me earlier, said he was coming by tomorrow to chill with us and wanted to talk with us about some things. Hmm..I wonder what? Anyway, c'mon chic..we going over one of my home girl's spot for some drinks and kicking it. I want to introduce you to her and she be cooking some bomb ass food..."

Chapter Twenty

Lorenzo awakened from his long, much needed nap feeling fully rejuvenated; he got up to rinse his face and brush his teeth. When done, he went downstairs to the kitchen to poured himself a glass of orange juice and proceeded into the living room, sitting on the couch, grabbing the remote and tuning in on Sports Center. Relaxing, he thought about the fellas up in the joint during football season. Football season in there meant a lot of shit talking, not to mention all the betting and football pools popping off.

He sure remembered those Sundays lying on his bunk glued to his 7" color television, sweating them pick 10 pool and parlay tickets, trying to win mad cartons of cigarettes and bags of commissary.

These memories made him decide to go ahead and write Z-man while he had some free time to catch him up on all that had been on in his world since his freedom. He went into his mother's computer room, grabbing a pen and writing pad, returned to the couch, where he then began writing his letter.

As Lorenzo wrote, he smiled, thinking of their friendship and the crazy times they had daily up in the joint, and how they ran the spades table in the cell block. They talked major shit when they had good hands, running dimes or Boston's on opposing teams. Prison wasn't a fun house, but they had to make due with their time after their classes in trade school were over for the day.

Lorenzo told Z-man about Alisha and his fling at the bus station; about Angelica being his main squeeze. He made sure to include all the juicy details of fucking Alisha, but not as much about Angelica because she was his number one. He let

Z-man know that he'll be sending him some pics soon.

Letter written, Lorenzo put the pen and writing pad off to the side, just sitting in thought for a few minutes. He planned to get a money order for $100.00 to send Z-man along with the letter, he knew how every dollar helped a man out big time while he was doing a bid.

Lorenzo now sat thinking what he was going to do for the rest of the day until Angelica got off work? He figured he'd head over to Mario's house and kick it with him for a few, get caught up on things happening out here on these streets so he'd know what was what.

Lorenzo went upstairs, slipped on his sneakers, closing his room door behind him as he left. As he headed out the front door, he checked his pocket to make sure he had his key, locking it behind him. He only had $150.00 dollars in his possession; he felt safer leaving the rest of his under his mattress.

Mario lived off Little Creek Road so Lorenzo caught the city public bus over to his place. It had been years since he rode the city bus, but he soon realized nothing about it had changed other than the cost of the fare. When he boarded, he noticed people standing because some of the passengers had their bags just sitting in empty seats, not bothering to move them so the passengers standing could sit down.

At one stop, a guy got on short of the fare; he and the driver got into an argument cause he refused to exit the bus which caused an uproar. People were trying to get to their destinations, some to work. One man became so angry and restless, he began walking up the isle toward the other guy at the front of the bus; other passengers followed. People were loud, shouting angrily at the man. When he saw the angry mob coming towards, he quickly exited the bus so the driver asked the passengers to please return to their seats and thanked them as well. The man gave the bus driver the middle finger as he walked off. Lorenzo just shook his head. Shortly after, Lorenzo rung the bell and seconds later exited the bus. Mario's house was only a block away.

Walking, Lorenzo crossed paths with two fine, thick ass females; one was a young dark skinned cutie, the other looked to be mixed with Black/PeurtoRican. He waited until they were a few feet past before turning to look at both their asses, shaking his head while whispering to himself, "Damn".

He reached Mario's apartment and knocked; a few seconds later, Mario's mother opened the door.

When she saw Lorenzo, she smiled and hugged him.

"Hello Lorenzo, I'm so glad you're home and out of that place. You've grown into a nice looking young man and you've gotten so big... please come in," Janet Banks stepped aside to allow him entrance.

"Hello Ms. Banks, thank you, and I'm so glad to be home as well. That isn't a place for any human being to be and I tried my best to stay as healthy as I could while in prison," Lorenzo told her.

"Yo Zo, what's up ace," Mario said as he came bounding down the stairs, giving Lorenzo some dap.

"Glad you came to check me out. Let's step out front so we can kick it homie," Mario told him. They stepped outside, deciding to take a little scroll around the neighborhood and reminisce on old times as well as discuss new beginnings.

"So, what's good playa.. what's your plans to get yourself back on track now that you a free man? I know you've just come home, but you can't waste time because you might miss an opportunity that was meant for you... know what I'm saying?" Mario told Lorenzo.

"Yeah you right ace. First thing is to go get my I.D., then I'm going to drop some apps in online and in person. I've already got a resume typed up.. I just hope I won't be overlooked cause I have a strike, criminal record...you feel me" answered Lorenzo.

" Yep, I know what you mean, but don't let that stagnate you cause they hiring felons out here major now. They understand people make mistakes plus some companies get tax cuts for hiring felons" Mario stressed.

Mario went on to say.

"I know a few people in high secured positions at their workplace that might could get you hired, some warehouses and some construction, plus, I'm going to talk to my supervisor at the warehouse plant where I work tomorrow to see if I can get you on..."

"Word! I appreciate that homie. I don't care what it is or pays as long as it's at least minimum wage or above, or what I got to do cause I'll take it. I'm trying to live right and work for mine! I know my blessings gone come as long as I'm trying to do right and live right," Lorenzo assured.

"Anyway, how's mom dukes doing and put me deep on this chic you was telling me about you kicking it with... and do she got any fine ass friends" asked Mario

Lorenzo laughed then went on to say,

"Mom dukes doing fine... she got this boyfriend she been with for some years now and he's cool. He's an old skool player type dude. Angelica, my lady friend, she's fine... and did I mention she's fine as hell... "

"...I stayed overnight at her place last night and it was the kind of welcome home you'd really appreciate, not to mention, she's an officer of the law" Lorenzo added.

"What homie? She a cop?! Well how in the hell did you pull that off? She must be a lame or she lonely as hell," Mario implied as he began laughing.

"Naw partna, she just seen this young, strong body of art looking so proper and couldn't let her trophy get away," Lorenzo replied then looked at Mario with a slight grin.

"Whatever yo... let's go over to the bar and shoot a few games of pool. I'm going to whip that ass some kind of proper," Mario assured.

Lorenzo replied, "you ain't gone whip shit, you can't ever hold a pole stick.. yo fingers too small..." they both broke into laughter as they headed to the pool hall.

When they reached the bar, the crowd was small; one pool table was opened out of the three that were there. Mario walked over to the bar station and gave the bar attendant a five dollar bill for five dollars in quarters to play at the pool table. They shot three games while talking smack to each other during every game. Lorenzo won all three games and in one game, Mario only got one shot before Lorenzo finished him off. Lorenzo then bought Mario and himself a plate of chicken wings and fries. They sat down at the bar eating while kicking it about life.

When they finished eating, Lorenzo gave the bartender a five dollar tip before they left the bar on their way back to Mario's house. About two hours passed while Lorenzo and Mario sat out front of the apartment building talking. Lorenzo asked Mario to use his cellphone; he called Angelica. The phone rang three times before she answered.

"Greetings Angelica speaking," she answered gleefully.

"Well hello there beautiful...how has your day been going today," Lorenzo asked?

Smiling, Angelica replied,

"Hey baby, my day been good, but it just got twenty times better now that I hear your voice. I've been thinking of you all day..."

"...Baby I have some good news and some bad news to tell you," Angelica mentioned to Lorenzo in a sad tone.

"Uh oh, let me hear the bad news first then the good" Lorenzo implied.

"The good news is that I'm getting off work early and I'm coming to get my baby so he can spend the rest of the day with me... and... the bad news is, tomorrow I have to leave the state because of a major break in a big drug case I'm following and assigned to and a major criminal been seen and located" Angelica told Lorenzo.

"I totally understand beautiful, but I'm over my best friend's house, will you come pick me up," Lorenzo asked

"What! Will I come pick you up? Don't make me kick yo ass asking a silly question...you in hot water when I see you sir! What's the address so I can put it in my GPS even though I know I don't need to," asked Angelica.

Lorenzo gave Angelica the address to Mario's and then confirmed that she was on her way.

"Mama got you on lock huh? Got to be in before the street lights come on or she gone beat that ass," Mario teased him.

"Fuck you dog, I'm Mandingo with my shit! She has to leave town soon on a case and wants to spend time with daddy before she leaves," Lorenzo said, with his chest puffed just a bit.

They were talking, laughing, and in such deep conversation, they didn't even notice Angelica pull up. Angelica got out of her truck and hollered out to Lorenzo.

"Hey motor mouth!"

Lorenzo turned around and smiled as soon as he saw his baby then blurted out.

"But somebody loves this mouth," as he walked up to her, hugging and kissing her. They both walked back over to where Mario was standing.

"Mario, this is Angelica, my beautiful new beginning," Lorenzo announce as he introduced her.

Mario went on to introduce himself.

"Hello, I'm Mario, Lorenzo's best friend. Nice to meet you... he's told me a lot about you."

"A pleasure to meet you Mario and I'm sorry to crash the party but Lorenzo has some duties to attend to right now," replied Angelica.

"Oh, no problem at all. I'll have plenty of time to chat with the homie...anyway give me a holla Lorenzo whenever time permits," Mario babbled.

"Mos Def," Lorenzo replied as he dapped up Mario then him and Angelica got in her truck, driving off.

"So what's our plans for the rest of the evening sexy," Lorenzo asked.

"Well, you and him..." as she reached over between his legs and gripped his manhood,

"...the two of you got some major, major work to put in tonight, but first we're going to stop at Pizza Hut and pick up the pizza I called in then we going home, shower, eat, then you gone put that work in," Angelica told Lorenzo.

"Hmm, I'm going to set sail to that there ship captain, knock sparks from that ass," Lorenzo replied.

Laughing out loud Angelica then blurted out, "boy you ass ain't got no sense whatsoever..."

As Angelica pulled into Pizza Hut's parking lot, she told Lorenzo she was just going to dash in to pay for and retrieve the pizza. Afterwards, she pulled off, in route to her house; they both were silent the entire way there.

As soon as Lorenzo closed the door and locked it, he put the pizza down on the living room table, pulling Angelica gently into his arms and devouring her lips with his own while rubbing, squeezing, and smacking her ass. Angelica let out a soft whimper then unlocked lips with Lorenzo and said,

"Oh hell no, report your ass to the shower right this minute sir."

Lorenzo followed Angelica to the shower where she set the water temperature, they both stripped and got in. In the shower Angelica backed herself up against Lorenzo's body. He wrapped his arms around her, softly squeezing her tits while leaning his head down, placing kisses on the back of her neck. Angelica, with eyes closed, softly moaned the moment she felt Lorenzo's tongue touch her neck and his hard manhood swelling up against her ass; it lit a fire inside her. Her body became hot as her love cave began throbbing, wanting his love muscle inside right that minute.

Lorenzo slid one hand slowly down Angelica's stomach and between her thighs to the lips of her love cave, massaging them lightly with his fingers as he continued to suck on her neck and nibble on her ears. Angelica became so horny, wanting to feel him inside her so bad, she began pressing her ass against his rock; creating all kinds of feelings within Lorenzo's body.

She turned around to face him, kissing him down his chest to his sack and started massaging it with her tongue while looking up at Lorenzo to watch his facial expressions, as she cupped his entire sack in her mouth.

Within the blink of an eye, she wrapped her warm mouth around his manhood and Lorenzo knees almost buckled under him. He grabbed Angelica's shoulder as she gave him some explosive head. Lorenzo, moaning loudly, just couldn't resist any longer; he needed to be inside her now. He somehow found the strength to reach down and stand Angelica up as they indulged in some heavy kissing.

He then picked her up with both hands and held her by her ass as his love muscle found its own way between her thighs and deep into her hot world of love. Angelica, with her arms and legs wrapped around Lorenzo, leaned back in mid air, Lorenzo delivering deep powerful strokes into her love cave as she cried out in pure pleasure; digging her nails into his back and at times, biting him softly on his shoulders.

As he pounded away, his love missile soon became full and he exploded, releasing his entire load deep within her world of love

*********************.

Relaxed and laying in bed eating pizza, Angelica reached over into the nightstand drawer on the side of the bed and pulled out a brand new android with the number written down on an index card; she handed these items to Lorenzo. He smiled, kissed and thanked her because he was about to buy a cellphone soon. Done eating, they just laid in bed in each others arms as they both fell sound asleep.

Hours passed by, it was now 11:42 am in the morning and Lorenzo had just awakened. He looked down, staring at Angelica and she had the biggest smile on her face.

"Well good morning, and what you smiling so hard for," Lorenzo asked

"Baaaaby! I've been woke for about two hours now, trying to get out of this damn bed and haven't moved an inch... I feel like I don't have no energy and I blame yo ass and his ass," Angelica replied as she grabbed Lorenzo's manhood.

"You better watch how you talk to him cause he's sensitive and will catch an attitude quick and you won't like him when he's angry," responded Lorenzo.

"Anyway, let's shower and get dressed so we can go eat some late breakfast at mom's house, and finally introduce you to her before you leave today, you are going to be her daughter in law one day," Lorenzo told Angelica.

Angelica looked at Lorenzo and smiled, then said.

"Yes, I'm truly in dying need of a warm shower to massage this body right now. "

They both got up and together headed to the shower so they could head over to his mother's house.

Out the shower and dressed, both Angelica and Lorenzo headed out the door together. In the truck, Angelica and Lorenzo shared a few jokes and laughs with each other. Angelica knew that she had fallen hard for Lorenzo because this very minute, in her mind, she was already picturing seeing him when she returns back home from duty.

As they pulled up in front of his mother's house, Angelica began to feel a little nervous. She really didn't know what to expect from Lorenzo's mother, being that she's a retired prosecutor and a damn good one. She wondered would she even approve of her being with her son knowing the way she loved, cared for and protected him.

"C'mon beautiful...don't worry, my mother is going to love you...trust me," Lorenzo assured Angelica. This made Angelica feel a lot better, but it didn't put an end to her nervousness one bit, it sort of enhanced it.

Lorenzo took Angelica by the hand as they walked up to the door, it was open so they entered. Lorenzo's mother and Thatcher were cuddled up together on the couch in the living room just enjoying each other's company as they watched the movie How Stella Got Her Groove Back.

"Hello mother, and hello Thatcher" Lorenzo greeted, as both him and Angelica entered the room.

"Hello there son and who may this nice looking young lady be?" his mother asked

"Hello, I'm Angelica and it's a pleasure to meet you Mrs. Barnes.   I've heard so much about you.

"This fine, stand up gentleman next to her is Mr. Conway, the only other man in my mother's life other than yours truly" Lorenzo said.

"It's an honor to meet you Angelica, you got a good guy there now" Thatcher told Angelica.

"How was the show mom? I know you two enjoyed yourselves" Lorenzo gave Thatcher some dap.

"Oh, the show was nothing short of amazing! They still got it, brought back a lot of great memories" Gina Mae answered.

"Mom, Angelica's an officer of the law...a Sergeant down at her precinct and she's about to leave town for a few on a case..." Lorenzo explained to his mother.

"Well, in that case, let's go into the kitchen Angelica. I have some breakfast left over from earlier, I can warm you up a plate and we can drink us a nice hot cup of coffee while we learn a little bit about each other. I'm very interested in knowing how you like your career" Gina Mae said to Angelica.

They left in the direction of the kitchen and Lorenzo took a seat on the couch. He and Thatcher talked about life, relationships, and laughed at some of the humorous stories they both shared with each other. In the kitchen, Angelica and Gina Mae sat at the kitchen table, getting to know one another over a cup of hot coffee.

"So Angelica, I don't want to know how you and my son met at this time, but he did tell me of your present career in law enforcement and I would like to talk about that if its okay with you" asked Gina Mae.

"Oh, it's perfectly fine with me Mrs. Barnes. Lorenzo also told me that you are a retired prosecutor; I wanted to gain much knowledge from you of your profession as well," Angelica replied.

"How long have you been an officer and what sparked your interest in your career of choice?" asked Gina Mae.

"Years ago, I lost my mother, father, and sister in a fatal car accident... they were killed by a drunken driver. I carried that pain for so long and wanted to help serve my city by trying to clean it up along with trying to help fight crime. I've been a police officer for five years now... I'm actually a Sergeant " Angelica told Gina Mae with pride.

Gina Mae nodded her head in approval, liking what she was hearing so far.

"As for myself, I've been retired about four and a half years now, I gave twenty-five dedicated years to my profession...and...I am sorry to hear about your family...that had to be hard on you..." She spoke these words with genuine concern.

Gina Mae went on to say,

"...When Lorenzo himself had a little incident with the law and was sentenced to serve ten years in state prison, it destroyed me inside. Five years into serving his time, I just got tired and threw the gloves in... I needed to be away from my line of work permanently, so I retired."

"I want to put in 25 years or better in my field myself. I'm also hoping to be married with children and a wonderful husband before all is said and done," Angelica stated then smiled.

"Sounds like a great plan Angelica and I'm available to talk if you ever want or need to. Hopefully, you'll be the daughter-in-law that gives me some grandchildren to spoil..." Gina Mae hinted while winking her eye.

She continued.

"Angelica, you really seem to be a very sweet person and by talking with you, I know you would be the best wife and mother.. Plus, with you, I'll know that big head son of mine will always be in the best of hands..."

Angelica gushed sweetly.

"Thank you and you're a very nice person as well. I love your guidance and it would be such an honor to call you mother-in-law one day in the near future..."

Finished with their coffee, Gina Mae placed both cups in the dishwasher and they headed back into the living room, rejoining Thatcher and Lorenzo, who were deep in conversation as they entered.

"Well, I hate I have to leave so soon but I must get going. I have to meet my partners at the station soon and prepare for this trip, but when I'm back in town, Ms. Barnes and Mr. Thatcher, we have a dinner date on me," Angelica assured them both.

She then hugged and thanked them for a wonderful first meeting and introduction.

"I'm going to walk you to your car Angelica," insisted Lorenzo.

Lorenzo and Angelica walked to her car. As soon as Angelica stopped and turned around, Lorenzo wrapped his arms around her waist, pulling her against him with his hands palming her juicy, round ass as he began kissing, sucking, and tasting her lips. When Lorenzo finally let her go, she caught her breath, whispering,

"I'm going to miss you soooo much baby, and the way you make me feel inside when them hands of yours are touching me, damn, damn, damn... "

"I'm going to miss you more, but I'll be right here waiting until my baby returns. Plus, we'll be talking on the phone as much as we can I'm sure," Lorenzo assured.

Angelica gave Lorenzo another hug and long passionate kiss, got in her truck and drove off. Lorenzo stood there a minute after she was gone then turned and headed back into the house. As soon as he was in the house, his mother looked at him and smiled.

"I really like her; she's very sweet, career oriented, and by the way she stares at you, I clearly can tell she has a love jones for you," Gina Mae told Lorenzo then giggled in a soft tone.

She then babbled on.

"Oh, I almost forgot... a letter came in the mail for you today from some woman. I saw the name on the envelope; it's over there on top of the television..."

Gina Mae had a little something extra she needed to add.

"...Son, you're a grown man now and I can't tell you "how to" in your friendships or relationships with these young ladies, but please be careful, because I'm telling you right now, there's no worst fury than a woman scorned..."

Lorenzo looked his mom into her eyes and replied,

"Yes ma'am."

Lorenzo grabbed the letter and went upstairs to his room, closing and locking the door behind him. He took off his shoes, put them neatly in his closet, got undressed and put on his sweatpants to feel more comfortable. He laid back on his bed to see who the letter could possibly be from as well as what it said. His eyes opened wide when he saw the name in the left corner of the envelope: it was from Alisha.

Lorenzo smiled extra hard as he quickly opened the envelope to retrieve the letter and from the big grin on his face, you would have thought its contents contained a check written out to him in a large sum of money. He pulled the letter out of the envelope and began to read it.

At the end of the letter, Alisha left a phone number for him to contact her; she really wanted to hear his voice. Lorenzo put the letter back in the envelope, laid back on the bed as he planned to give Alisha a call in a few. He just wanted to relax for a few.

Two and a half hours passed before Lorenzo got up to give Alisha that call and he couldn't wait to speak with her. He went downstairs, grabbed the cordless house phone and dialed Alisha's number. The phone rang twice before she picked up.

"Hello, this is Alisha speaking," Alisha mumbled as she began to get up out of bed from a long night of fun and drinks with Sasha over one of her friend's house. Who the hell could this be she pondered, still a bit hung over.

"Well, hey there sexy, how's everything going with your transition back home..." Lorenzo asked.

It was time to find out how she was doing, how she was treating that bomb ass pussy and how the hell she had gotten her hands on his Mom's address???

About The Author

Jason Beckett was born in Norfolk, Virginia and raised in the neighborhoods of Lambert's Point and Park Place. His mother, a hard working woman, raised him and his three siblings all by her lonesome, he is the second oldest sibling.

His mother was a nurse working two jobs to provide for her family therefore she was rarely home but always managed to have their meals prepared. Although times were extremely hard, his mother always found a way to provide just enough.

Jason, with no father figure in his life to teach him how to grow into a man, a gentleman, developed internal anger from his father never wanting to be a part of his young childhood, so he decided to go out into the rough neighborhoods he lived in and acquire friends that helped release some of his pain.

Hanging in the streets, creating all kinds of mischief, landed him behind bars serving a ten year prison sentence. It was behind those prison walls that he went to school and acquired a Certification in Data Entry of Computers. It was also behind those walls that Jason discovered his gift, love and passion for writing; the gift God had given him. He used writing as a way to release his anger and deepest feeling on paper. He also gained a love of books and that's where he fell in love with poetry, after reading "**Poems by Maya Angelou**."

That book lit the poetry fire in him and brought out the poet within waiting to be heard. He fell in love with *Maya Angelou* and her compassion for people; her strength, her words of power, but most of all, the poem uplifted him and paved the way to writing his very own poetry, in his own words of power.

Jason Beckett's first book to be published was "**Poetic Rotationz**."

Author Jason Beckett

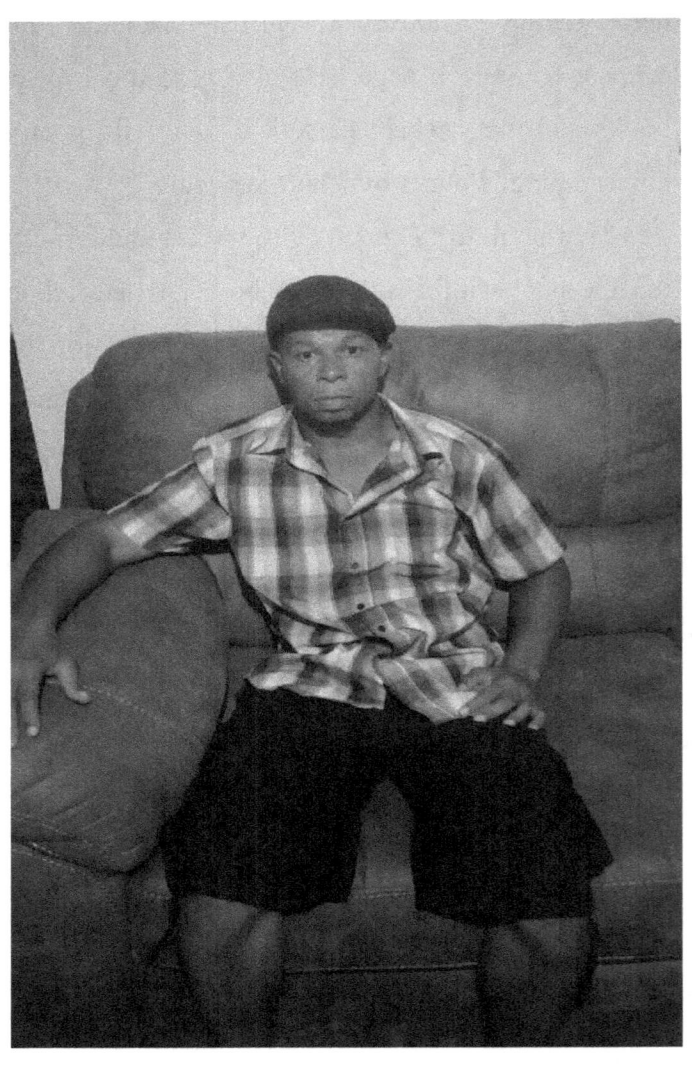

www.ingramcontent.com/pod-product-compliance
Lightning Source LLC
Chambersburg PA
CBHW070554130626
46556CB00001B/159